AT LAST, JACK HAD COME!

Bogie stood, waiting to hear Jack's voice broadcast. But the com lines stayed quiet, except for a static chittering that he could not comprehend. The coracle quivered as if buffeted by a wind or tide and he could hear that it had been taken in, that it was now docked in a hold of some kind. Outside, vacuum was being bled away and air pumped in.

He faced the main air lock, anticipating its opening. His mission as a signpost to Colin's whereabouts was nearly fulfilled, but even more important, the expectation of a reunion with Jack warmed him. War had torn them away from each other, but Bogie had never doubted that fate would bring them together again. Helmet visor forward, he scanned the portal eagerly.

But it was not opened, it was blown away. Bogie's armor rocked back on its heels, sensors flooded by heat and the blast—and the nightmare Kabuki-mask faces of the invaders as they climbed in, their chitin aglow in the explosion's wake.

He'd been found all right, but by the Thraks. . . .

DAW Titles by Charles Ingrid

CHARLES INGRID
THE
SAND WARS
CHALLENGE MET
6

DAW BOOKS, INC.
DONALD A. WOLLHEIM, PUBLISHER

375 Hudson Street, New York, NY 10014

First Printing, August 1990

1 2 3 4 5 6 7 8 9

PRINTED IN THE U.S.A.

To Vincent DiFate
This one's for you, Vinnie, intrepid
interpreter of word to vision.
Thanks.

Prologue

The vehicle was little more than a coracle, thrown to the mercy of solar winds and planetary gravities. A man stood at the heavily shielded port watching the heavens pass. Intently, he viewed the planet the vehicle orbited. It was aswirl with clouds, but he could see the burned off continents through rifts in the cover. The blue of water and white-blue of cloud obscured most of the damage, yet he could see streaks of green and brown coming through. Initial reports from his far-flung organization told him that there were possibilities here once more. Clean water, grass, seedlings, along with the ores. The norcite would bring them back, if nothing else. *Resurrection*, he thought, and the thought tipped the corners of a weary smile. The expression smudged out the worry lines.

He was older, his shoulders bowed with fatigue. He wore the plain jumpsuit of the working class, a miner's suit, the trouser section lined with pockets both full and empty. Over its drab colors, he wore the deep blue, long vested overrobe of his office. A rough-hewn cross rested upon his chest, rising and falling with each breath. His hair, thinning brown strands across his broad skull, had been thick once and more tinted with auburn than it was now. Only his eyes remained the same: vigorous, alive, the deepest of browns, windows to a soul still fiery with conviction.

"Jack would be proud," he voiced aloud. "He's brought a planet back to life." He'd had to bring an emperor to his knees to do it, but the resurrection had begun. Colin watched the planet avidly, drinking in its phoenix rebirth out of ashes.

He was dwarfed by the massive battle armor behind him, its opalescent Flexalinks catching the light as it shifted nearer. "Should have brought Jack," said the armor, its voice sounding forth in magnificent basso profundo tones.

The man did not take his gaze from the portal. The armor was not empty, though it should have been, and the voice did not come from a human throat nor a computer sentience. There was alien flesh inside the armor, regenerating like a chick within its shell. That it missed the soldier who wore the armor, its symbiotic link, gave it more credence than Colin had at one time supposed.

The Walker saint replied, "Jack's busy. He'll come after us." The man did not elaborate. The machinations of humankind might stall any kind of rescue, but Colin had been prepared for that.

It appeared the armor was not. "You should have brought Jack," it repeated with the petulance of a small child. It shifted and brought up a gauntlet. The massive fist could easily crush Colin, but he did not flinch as it came to rest upon his shoulder. The petulant tone faded. "There," Bogie said. "Company."

The armor's sensors were far better than human eyes and so it was a while before Colin could see what the other registered. Then, when he recognized it, it was with a sucked in breath. His right hand went involuntarily to his cross and gripped it.

"By God," Colin whispered. "I was right."

The cross within his fist cut into his weathered palm. God was his business, not diplomacy. But it had seemed to him that mankind had no right to war with a creature they had not even met face-to-face, as terrible as that enemy had proven in the past. He was old enough to know destiny when it crossed his path.

The heavens seemed to tremble as the alien fleet moved into sight, warships thrumming with massive power. The tiny rescue coracle would be dwarfed by any vessel they sent out. Colin looked out over the fleet even as a lethal, viperous looking vehicle peeled away and headed in their direction. To have been spotted so quickly!

Colin dropped the cross and laid his hand over the gauntlet on his shoulder. "I can't take you with me," he said.

Armor couldn't flinch . . . could it?

"Alone again?" said the being.

"'Till Jack finds you. He should. But I can't take you with me." To meet with them, to have at last the evidence his Protestant ministry had long searched for, to prove to the worlds and mankind that Christ had indeed gone on to walk on other shores. There wasn't an archaeological site the Walkers delved where they hadn't also found signs of these others. They had become, enemy or not, someone he had to treaty with. Yet, as the fighter winged toward him, his dreams failed and his heart skipped a beat. What if he was wrong?

As if echoing his thoughts, Bogie growled. "The enemy."

"No," Colin murmured. "The unknown." He took a steadying breath. "You're my signpost, Bogie. You have to tell what I've told you, and point the way after. *If I'm very, very fortunate, I'll be there to meet you at road's end.*"

The coracle rocked as a tractor beam locked about it.

Chapter 1

The sound of being locked into a berth rang throughout the ship. Its clamor vibrated through the ship's skeleton as though it were a bell tolling the end of a journey, the attainment of a destination. After weeks shipbound, in vacuum and in FTL warp, the noise echoing through normal atmospheric pressure was deafening—and welcome.

The recycler began to shut down as the locks were opened to pump in fresh air. Jack's ears popped as the pressure changed and he swung about in the passenger lounge chair. He looked at his fellow traveler though her amber hair waving down across one shoulder hid the expression on her fine-boned profile.

"Now," he said. "The emperor shows his true colors."

The young woman could not hide her shudder from him. She looked about the cabin as she turned to him, her gaze surveying the lounge as if worried they might be spied upon, and she answered quietly, "I think you already have him scoped. We're still his prisoners."

"Maybe." He could not contain his growing excitement. "I beat him to a standstill as half a man. Think what I could do completed."

She turned back to the viewing screen, even though it had been shut down and the lounge portal was still locked for deep space. Jack felt her closeness as though she actually leaned against him with her head upon his shoulder, for she had not withdrawn her intimacy, and he felt himself smile.

The door to the lounge room opened with a faint hissing noise, and the emperor stepped through. The man was slight and wiry, fair-skinned and heavily freckled, his frizzled red hair alive with an electrical aura of its own, and the sharp gaze of his cat-green eyes rested upon Jack.

"Commander Storm," Emperor Pepys said, in a deep tone that belied his slight body. "Until you have been decommissioned, I suggest you rise and salute your emperor."

Jack Storm paused, and then, slowly and deliberately, he rose and saluted. He stood head and shoulders and then some over the older man, and if he'd been encased in his battle armor, he would have towered over Pepys, filling the entire room with his presence. The two men locked gazes, and Pepys turned away first, unable to stay with the clear as rainwater faded blue eyes of the other. The corner of Jack's mouth twitched. He remained standing.

"I've sent for an escort," Pepys said. He plucked an imaginary thread from the seams of his red and gold jumpsuit which was not his customary elegant wear but far more suitable for the journey they'd just made.

"Escort?" Amber echoed. "Or guard?"

Pepys' face twisted in ill-concealed anger. He shoved a fist into his right leg pocket. "Does it matter? You agreed to return with me, and this is my world."

Amber's lips curved shut and she said nothing although she might well have reminded him Malthen was her world, too. But it wasn't in the sense that she came from the underground, from the unprivileged society, and Malthen had never held anything for her, until it had brought her Jack.

"No Thraks," Jack said, and he moved to the back of her chair, his protection of her obvious for all that it was unspoken.

The emperor's anger became wry amusement. "Ah, yes," he said. "Let us not forget the phobia which drove you away from my Knights. Whatever else we may do here, I won't have you upsetting the alliance which I have taken such pains to reweave."

"Alliance. You've been infiltrated and conquered, but you're too blind to see it." Jack's hands, resting on the back of Amber's chair, touching but not hidden by the cascade of her hair, tightened. "They've sucked you in."

"There are considerations you know nothing of."

"If you'd care to elaborate, I'd like to know just what you've been planning."

Pepys made an exasperated sound, his lips pursed. He took his hand out of his pocket and slapped it on the bulkhead, then keyed open the com lines to the bridge. "Raise the shields."

"But, sire—"

"Riot watch notwithstanding—do as I say!"

The portal shield before Amber began to rise,

and Malthen's white-gold sunlight flooded in, made bearable by the window filter. Pepys pointed outside, beyond the berth cradle, across the spaceport. Jack turned his head, and his eyes narrowed.

"It's the Walkers. They've heard my private ship was berthing today—they've come to see if I've brought back their saint." Pepys' voice was faint and bitter. "He brought me to this."

Jack straightened. A riot guard, faintly seen, but still visible at the perimeters of the landing field jostled against a wall of flesh. He could not hear the voices at this range, but the sight of Thraks in riot gear and battle armor controlling ordinary people made his flesh prickle. "They know St. Colin's missing?"

"Yes, damn it all. Word broke out while we were en route. I could not have kept it quiet much longer anyway, but I had hoped for better." Pepys stepped up, joining them at the window. "Old friend," he said quietly. "Is this the legacy you wanted to leave?"

Jack had often seen fiery indignation in Colin's mild brown eyes, but he knew the Walker leader would never want a religious war in his name. The Walker religion had been embraced for its benevolent tenets as well as its search for new worlds that Christ might have visited. It was as tolerant as any religion he knew, though he did not espouse it. The fervor he saw now, the wave of humanity dashing itself against the riot shields and inflexible, beetlelike carapaces of the Thraks, bore no resemblance to anything he'd ever heard Colin preach.

He started to say something as he turned to

Pepys, but the emperor was still fixed on the sight before them, and interrupted Jack, saying, "So you may call my honorable Knights an escort or a guard or whatever you wish—but we're not leaving here without them. We'll never get through otherwise." Pepys backed away from the window. With a snap, he added, "You've agreed to find Colin for me. Cross me now, and you'll not only be court-martialed for the treasonous acts you've committed and been taken prisoner for—you'll be the one responsible for the slaughter that follows."

The emperor left abruptly. Amber tilted her head, waiting until the fall of his steps could no longer be heard. Then she said, "Nice man."

Jack made a noncommittal sound. He unclenched his hands from the back of her chair and moved them to the back of her neck, where he stroked soft and fragrant skin. "A fine pair we are," he told her. "A treasonous Knight and a thief."

She laughed and raised her arms so that she might grasp his hands. "A thief and an assassin," she corrected. "But you've never betrayed your Knighthood." Her voice sharpened. "Pepys corrupted it—corrupted them all." Her words were spat out, venomous and bitter.

He leaned over her. "Witch."

She tilted her head back, throat arching gracefully. "Hero."

Jack shook his head, laughing so softly that when she met his mouth with a kiss, she was surprised to feel the laughter vibrating pleasantly in his lips.

Springtime had come to Malthen and its underbelly, the slums known simply as under-Malthen. Green shoots ignored the still gray skies and slanting drizzle as the freezing rains of winter warmed. They pushed their insistent growth upward, fracturing concrete and perma-plast. Only the rose-pink obsidite walls of the emperor's residence, the palace of the Triad Throne, could deny them life. Here the grass retreated and settled to a life of surrender in the lawns and grounds, which was a far better fate than that which it faced on the Training grounds. No matter how brave the grass or weed, it was destroyed when hard-heeled boots of Flexalink ground it to dust. It grew relentlessly, only to be trampled by battle armor.

This day it had a respite, and pushed through the first wet splatters of rain, ignorant of its fate.

Lassaday, first sergeant of the Dominion Knights, first D.I. of the Malthen training station, his chunky body as hard as the Flexalinks worn by a Knight, his bald head darkened and weathered by the usual Malthen sunshine, hung his elbows over the observation railing and spat in disgust. The grounds were empty, on a day when the veterans and recruits should have been drilling, ill-weather or not. The Walker riots confined them all to base and he had little choice about his assignments. He could only thank his lucky stars that it had brought out the Thraks first, Minister Vandover taking advantage of the human fearfulness of the aliens to keep the dissenters at bay.

The sergeant looked over the pitted and battle-scarred retaining walls. His cheek bulged with the wad of stim he chewed and he spat another mud-like droplet over the railing when the alert came in over the com line. He answered it, taking his orders gruffly, and keyed off. He pulled back from the railing after a last look at the acreage before him and went downstairs.

The shop was as empty as the grounds, racks of battle armor in repair hanging silent. The locker rooms, permeated by an odor of fear as palpable as the odor of sweat, were vacant except for the robosweep, squeaking as it toured the aisles in its janitorial mode. Lassaday strode through, aware of the cameras following him as he made his own sentry rounds. He heaved a sigh as he broke into the fresh air once again.

The barracks, however, teemed with activity as Lassaday approached them. Recruits and veterans sat in knots, polishing their minor equipment—bracers, gauntlets, small arms—or they stood around idly gossiping.

"Th' emperor's ship is ported. I want an honor guard of twelve volunteers, and I'm only takin' th' best of you." It was an assignment he had feared, but he would take it, and he wanted only the top Knights beside him when he did.

The knots broke up, mumbling, arguing, and he could hear the drift of their voices, the same words, the same arguments that had driven him to the solitude of the Training grounds in the first place.

He'd heard enough. Anger swelled his bull chest, and when he bellowed it out, he didn't care who heard or heeded.

"I've had it! You've got a problem, bring it to me! Pepys has th' right to call an escort. We'll be bringin' him and Commander Storm in, and, by God, if he's gonna be judged, I want th' commander to be judged open of mind and free of doubt—not by a bunch of ball-less wonders." He stared around the compound which his bellow had brought to silence.

A young man, his chin clipped by a fresh laser scar, pink and lacy upon his skin, looked up from his workbench. "Sarge," he began. "We buried the man with full honors—now he's hauled back, alive and in irons."

Lassaday pointed a blunt finger. " 'Th'man,' " he repeated, "is your commander."

"Was," a voice rumbled from the shadowed interior beyond the barracks' doorway. "Now we've got a walking Milot furball for a commander."

There were shouts of protest including one young, clear voice saying, "K'rok's all right."

"He's alien!"

"You're kind of strange yourself," the recruit fired back, and the argument disintegrated into laughter.

Lassaday rubbed the ball of his thumb over his jaw. "Th'Milot's my commanding officer," he said, "and it's not fitting for me to talk ill of him, for all that he's part of the Thrakian League and we're Dominion and Triad here. But K'rok fills a commander's shoes and that's all that's required of him. You might do well to remember that when a Thraks goes to war, he takes no prisoners except for th' best—and K'rok's fought his way up through their ranks as well. And all that's required of you is a shut mouth and clear head when we meet Emperor Pepys. Jack Storm was a good man to all of us—the last true Dominion Knight, he is, and he deserves respect."

"Traitor," someone said, but Lassaday's piercing dark stare could not pick out the voice's owner.

His cheek bulged for a moment as if he chewed out his thoughts before he spoke. Then, reluctantly, "Some say so. But it's not been proved to me yet."

"Then why'd he fake his death and leave?"

Another recruit added, "And he lost his armor."

The growing clamor quieted at that. Someone said, "Is it true? Did he lose his armor?"

Lassaday spat to one side, scattering recruits. Then, "Yes. That much is true."

No suit, no soldier. They'd been drilled with that since the day they'd been accepted into Emperor Pepys' resurrected Knights. Those of them who'd made it this far into the service shivered as they thought of being without their Flexalink skins, their weapons, their second selves. *He'd lost his armor.* That alone was tantamount to treason.

"We can't judge what happened," Lassaday said, his gravelly voice low. "Not until we hear th' story."

A slender man moved into the doorway, and leaned against it, his captain's bars winking on his shoulder. Travellini met the sergeant's stare as he said, "And what if Pepys doesn't allow us to hear it?"

The NCO rocked back on his heels slightly at the unthinkable. "No," he answered. "That wouldn't be."

The captain traced a seam down the outside of his slacks and flicked off a piece of lint or dust. He looked up. "Nothing says Pepys has to give Jack a military court-martial. It wouldn't be the first time Storm has been betrayed by the system."

A freckle-faced recruit crouching over his boots, applying a patina like that of stainless steel, blurted out, "That's not fair."

The Dominion captain's mouth twisted at one corner as he answered, "None of us are likely to ever learn what drove Commander Storm away from here—and what brought him back. And we dare not judge him until, as the old troopers like to say, we've walked in his boots."

"Amen," echoed Lassaday, his anger soothed by the captain's calmness. The knots of men began to break up, voices quieted now, tones somber. Never before had one of their own been brought back in shackles, bereft of his armor, rumors of treason and cowardice hanging over his head.

But then, the aged sergeant thought, none of their own had ever dared to fight both the enemy and the emperor. He braced himself. "Now, all right, you spineless excuses for Knights. Which ones of you are goin' with me in escort?"

Rawlins stepped out of the shadows. Lassaday felt a prickle of apprehension run through him. He was a copy of Storm, but a pure copy undulled by time or cynicism, hair the color of winter wheat and blue eyes with an electric intensity in them, a copy that rang truer than its original because life had not yet defeated Rawlins. But the boy had never been the same since the military action on Bythia that had entangled his life with Storm's and with the Walker Colin's. Rawlins had served as the commander's aide-de-camp and as for the Walker saint, it was said that Colin had blessed the boy, cursed the boy, and even raised him from the dead.

"Sergeant," Rawlins said softly. "I'd like to volunteer for detail."

Though he had misgivings, there was no way Lassaday could gainsay the lieutenant. He gave a short, abrupt nod. "That's it, then. Who is going with me and th' lieutenant?" He was not surprised to have to turn them away in droves, if only because there was a maudlin curiosity to see the legendary Jack Storm.

Amber was the first to see them crossing the riot lines, on foot, in full battle armor, Malthen sunlight glinting off the Flexalinks. They had not been able to bring the transports through the still pressing crowds of Walkers and other protesters. She stood up even as Pepys came into the lounge. "They're here," she said gently.

Jack had been sitting in repose, eyes closed, faint lines smoothed upon his brow. Years of cold sleep suspension had kept him much younger than his chronological age. His sandy hair was a little higher off his forehead than it had been, the laugh lines at the corners of his eyes a little deeper, and the grooves about his mouth sharper than she remembered, but his was a body still well in its prime. He looked up as a clink sounded from Pepys' hands, and his waking gaze fell on the shackles his emperor held.

He said nothing, but Amber's heart twisted as the lines in his face deepened as his sovereign approached.

Chapter 2

Amber walked the palace hallway, ignoring the gaunt shadow her body threw upon the walls. She hugged herself against a chill that was born not of temperature but of spirit, an iciness the black silks she wore could not keep out. The sight at the port had stayed with her, no matter how hard she tried to pace it off: the wall of Thraks reared in opposition to a wall of human flesh, people crushing forward inexorably, demanding that their saint be returned to them. White-lipped, Pepys had greeted Baadluster, his Minister of War, and the honor guard had surrounded them, swallowing them up—and if it had not been for those machines of war, she did not think they would have made their transports.

They had had only one incident of any measure—and her own heart had thudded as they had approached the transports, and she could see a familiar face beyond the guards.

Baadluster had made a low sound in his throat as if he also recognized Denaro, militant right hand of the Walker church. "You should have taken that one out," he muttered to his emperor, "when you could have."

Jack acted as if he had not heard them, but his

chin went up, and his gaze met the flint dark one of the man standing beyond the Thraks. In a society where biological years often did not match years lived, because of cold sleep and other factors, men no longer measured actual ages. But they recognized *prime*, and each of them was in his. Jack had once taught Denaro to be a Knight, a wearer of battle armor.

In fear, Amber reached out and touched Jack's wrist, hoping to break their stares, for Denaro was heavily armed despite the large, hand-carved wooden cross hanging upon his chest. Her gesture had no effect and now Denaro was speaking, his voice cutting through the crowd noise as if it were a laser.

"You came back without him."

Jack stopped in his tracks and his escort slowed as well. A lesser man would have been dwarfed by the battle armor, but he was not. "Denaro," Jack responded. "If I had gone with him, he would have come back with me—or neither of us would have returned at all."

Denaro's eyes blinked slowly. He scorned to wear Walker overrobes, and his muscles flexed under his miners' jumpsuit.

"Jack!" Amber warned, even as Denaro's hand moved, but the crowd surged with a wild scream, as it caught her fear. The Thraks reared up, chitin and carapace pressing against the softer flesh of the rioters.

Something came hurtling through the air at them, moving so quickly that none of the guards could shift to catch it, even as Denaro shouted, "You serve a murderer!"

Jack shrugged off Amber's hand and snatched the object up, curling his fingers tightly about it.

As the tidal wave of security bore Denaro and the others away, the Walker shouted a last time. "Find him," he said. "And tell the truth. Or I'll do it for you."

Jack turned his hand over and opened his fist. A smaller, no less crude wooden cross rested in his palm. Amber sucked in her breath, recognizing it as one of St. Colin's. Jack looked out, searching for Denaro and no longer able to see him. He raised his hand in the air.

"I hear you, Denaro!"

The memory now chilled Amber. How close Denaro had come to inciting out-and-out riot. Pepys feared the Walkers. If not for their pressure, she and Jack would be dead now, but the emperor had a desperate need for them. Yet she knew the cloth Pepys and his minister had been cut from. Once Jack accomplished the impossible, if he could accomplish the impossible, the two of them would be discarded.

The hospital wing was deserted, a seldom used area of the palace, maintained only to preserve the health of the emperor. She paused at the clinic doorway, knowing she could jimmy the palm lock if she had to, but also knowing that the prisoner within was honor bound to stay imprisoned and that he had made her vow as well. That she thought him a fool made no difference in how much she loved and worried about him.

A noise in the hallway brought her up short. She thought she heard a scrabble, a clacking of carapaces against the obsidite flooring—and even as the hairs on the back of her neck prickled, the noise faded. When a man rounded the juncture and approached her, a tall, homely man with pasty skin, lank brown hair, and lips too thick to smile appealingly, she spat at him.

"No Thraks! You promised no Thraks on the guard duty."

Vandover Baadluster gave an ironic bow. "And good afternoon to you as well, Milady Amber. What need do the emperor and I have of guards with you on duty?"

She could feel the color blaze in her cheeks as she answered, "I won't have the bugs within eye-shot or earshot of me and Jack. May I congratulate you on your handling of our allies. We couldn't be more rife with them. You have rolled over, belly up, and surrendered."

"Harsh words from a beautiful whore," Vandover said mildly, but there was nothing mild about the flint dark eyes that blazed out of his pale face. "If you wish to worry about alien contact, I suggest you worry about the Ash-farel. The Thraks, at least, we have met face-to-face and can bargain with. The Ash-farel are like a black hole, swallowing worlds and colonies never to be seen again."

She said nothing in answer to that, but turned away, her short cape billowing with the disdain she felt. She could feel her heart hammering in her chest, but the man did not bait her further.

Instead, he seemed to be examining the windowless door as if he could see through its panels. "The doctors should be done with him soon. I came down to tell you the tape has been updated successfully."

The hammering faltered badly. She swallowed to hide the flutter of pain it caused. "Then there's nothing to stop the imprinting."

"Nothing but Commander Storm himself, if the doctors pass him." Vandover turned, aware that he'd drawn her attention back to him.

Amber met his burning stare defiantly. She said nothing.

The minister thinned his lips with a semblance of a smile. "The mind-loop of a seventeen-year-long cold sleep must be a formidable experience. I myself find it hard to believe that he volunteered for this. A most unusual reward for the task Pepys has asked of him, don't you think?"

Amber could feel her emotions seething, boiling just under her skin, but she lifted her chin and said coldly, "You might find it . . . difficult. Jack might find it gratifying."

Vandover laced his fingers together. They made a pale steeple against the unrelieved darkness of his robes. "Never doubt that Pepys wants Colin found. No one wishes the holy war of revenge that will result unless the man is brought back. Even I." He paused a moment longer. "I came to ask you for your aid."

"Me? What could you possibly want from me?"

"Commander Storm's passion to regain his past is second only to his passion for you. I want you to sway him, milady. Convince him that he may be crippling himself by imprinting the tape before he undertakes his mission to find St. Colin. Convince him to wait . . . until later."

Or until you can destroy the tape, Amber thought, but did not say aloud. "We went through hell to find this tape."

"Indeed. Through that and Green Shirts. . . ." Vandover paused, as though naming yet another dissident faction left a bad taste in his mouth. "And it is, unless I am mistaken, a tape of a man going through yet another hell. We need Commander Storm sound in mind and body."

"St. Colin has disappeared so well that not one of the thousand under-ministers of his church know where he could possibly be. I don't think I can ask Jack not to have his memories restored before he goes after him. It wouldn't be fair . . . I couldn't do that to him." Amber fought a desperate battle to keep her voice cool, free of emotion. If Vandover wanted him to avoid the tape, all the more reason Jack needed it.

She would not let herself look at Baadluster, but she knew he watched her avidly. She could feel his stare burning into her.

"And what about you, milady? Is it a chance you want him to take? Will you chance losing him? An imprint from a year or two ago is nothing—but this—his memories may not integrate. He may remember his life then, and nothing now. What of you, Amber? Are you ready and willing to be forgotten?"

She clenched her teeth. *Jack would not, could not, forget her.* But her mind trembled at the thought. Rather than give Baadluster the satisfaction of knowing he'd shaken her, she said nothing.

Baadluster waited long silent moments, then gave a bleak smile. "We are allies, Milady Amber, uneasy confederates, perhaps, but entangled nonetheless. I urge you to be selfish now, for whatever reasons you have, because we both desire the same result. Think on it." He paused another long moment, heard nothing forthcoming from Amber, turned on his heels and left with that hard smile still on his face.

She watched his back until he was no longer in view. Not until he was gone—as far from her senses as from her sight, did she let his words touch her.

Not that Jack had many choices in the future for himself or for her now. Perhaps Jack had been fighting Thraks so long that he was incapable of accepting their alliance—or perhaps he was right, and the mysterious, threatening Ash-farel was not the current enemy but a new race to be contacted and negotiated with despite their reputation as the Thraks' oldest and most deadly foe.

Amber let her thoughts sink into her despair. She was under no illusion that anything Jack did here and now was voluntary. What choice did they have? She knew the rumors permeating the ranks of his battalions. Coward. Traitor. Murderer. The emperor had brought him back in shackles.

Publicly Jack was dead. His emperor could do anything he wanted to Jack without fear of reprisal. But the man who thought that of Storm was greatly mistaken.

The panel before Amber opened suddenly, startling her and sending her thoughts scattering like dry leaves before a cold autumn wind. The emerging doctors blocked her view of Jack and they talked among themselves as they passed her, ignoring her presence.

"Remarkable condition, but I'd like to see those toe buds done before he leaves . . . the scar tissue will only continue to thicken until the point where we can't consider that option—"

"Forget the implants, he balances well enough without those digits. It's the mental profile that worries me, but for a man who was chilled down for more than half his lifetime, he spikes well enough, I guess. I wonder if Pepys knows what he's gotten into. . . ."

Their voices faded as they turned the corner and passed from view.

Amber turned her head slowly until the room opened up in front of her and she saw Jack sitting crookedly on a lab table, fastening the front of his tunic. Her senses flared with the sight of him, his plain but honest face unaware that she looked at him, his sandy hair darkened by exertion on the treadmill, his faded eyes focused on thoughts and events elsewhere, relaxed body still muscular from the demands of wearing battle armor. And although she'd grown up in the years she'd known him, he hadn't aged to speak of, his body, frozen by time, that of a man in his prime.

She spoke as she entered. "Vandover says your tape has been transcribed."

He looked up, not startled, having grown used to her catlike ways of entry and exit. He smiled, crinkling the sun wrinkles at the corners of his eyes. "It's going to work! I'm all cleared. Pepys should be down in a minute to discuss final arrangements." He reached out for her and pulled her close. She found it momentarily disconcerting—he sat on the lab table, and she looked down at him.

Biting down on her lip, she made a decision. "I saw Jonathan while you were in examination," she said.

Jonathan was Colin's right hand, a great big

bear of a man—and he was the only survivor of the Walker's ill-fated expedition. Jack looked up, meeting her worried gaze. "He's comatose," she added. "He may not make it."

"What happened?"

"They don't know . . . there's not a mark on him. He's around the corner with more security than I've seen in a long time. Jack . . . it's not like Colin to take Jonathan with him and then abandon him."

"You worry too much."

"You've given me a lot to worry about."

He kissed her chin, a nibble of a kiss. In a low, intimate voice that did not match his words, he said, "I'll want to see him before they wire me up for the cryo bay. They just told me they expect the playback imprint to run maybe four, five days."

"Pepys left word you're to be let in. I wouldn't." She swallowed. There was a heat creeping up her body, spreading from the point on her jaw where his lips rested briefly and then continued on, following the swan swoop of her neck down to the delicate bones below her throat where he paused again. She closed her eyes and, despite the attention Jack was giving her, she saw Jonathan's vast, near lifeless body, sheeted and wired, monitors projecting the reluctance of the life force it retained.

"Do you think Jonathan would mind waiting a few minutes?"

"Minutes?" she retorted. "You'd better take your time with me, soldier. And no, I don't think Jonathan would mind at all. He had a certain lust for life himself." And her eyes brimmed, in spite of herself. To combat the lump in her throat, she added, "I want you, too."

"There were times," Jack said softly, "on board ship when I thought I could hear you breathing on the other side of the cabin wall."

Amber shook her head. "If we'd been that close, they couldn't have kept me from you." She did not fight as he encircled his arms about her waist and drew her up on the exam table next to him, but she did grasp his right hand, his four-fingered hand, where the frostbite of cold sleep had taken away his little finger, and said, "Someone should do something about sealing this lab. We wouldn't want to break quarantine."

"I'll take care of that," and he voice-coded the lock with a phrase that made her laugh. And then he proceeded to do something very unorthodox to cool her fever.

For long moments, all the worlds and all the stars concentrated into the intimacy of two people entwined with one another.

Chapter 3

"I intercepted a message matrix from the Green Shirts," Vandover said, not bothering to conceal the pleased look which he knew contorted his fleshy lips.

Pepys, immersed in his control mesh, looked up with an irritated flash. "You know I'm busy."

"But not too busy for this, I trust." Vandover handed over the transcript which he had been tapping across the palm of one hand.

Pepys took it and scanned it. His red hair crackled with intensity as he asked, "When and where did you get this?"

"They attempted to pass it to Storm when we brought him through the port."

Pepys looked back down at the encoded and deciphered paper: *Situation with Walkers to be kept enflamed. Pepys needs to keep you alive.* He let the script slip through his fingers to the floor where it lay among a nest of cable wire. "Tell me something I don't know."

"We guessed. This confirms it."

"That the Green Shirts have a vested interest in Storm we've known for some time. Does Storm know a message failed to reach him?"

"I don't think so."

Pepys relaxed in his chair. An abstract expression passed over his freckled face as he listened to his com net, all the while talking to his Minister of War. "Send the word out through the usual informers that continued rioting will diminish Storm's use to me, not increase it. There may come a time when I choose to quash civil rebellion instead of cater to it."

"Yes, sire. About the girl?"

"She keeps him happy for the moment. We'll discuss her options later."

Vandover nodded. He backed toward the doorway.

"Vandover."

Baadluster stopped. "Yes, sire?"

"We know that Jack's mind-loop was retrieved through Madam Sadie. That means she was storing it in her private vaults, probably as collateral for one of her private loans. Any idea for whom?"

"Not yet."

"It's vital."

Vandover answered with only a terse nod. Pepys swiveled in his chair, a pendulum of nervous energy. Their eyes met briefly.

"The Dominion has contacted me. The president is seeking to renegotiate the interest on their loan. Financing a war effort has proven to be more expensive than they anticipated. But he has also asked for a starfleet increase and for two more battle armor units."

Vandover's dark eyes grew bright. "We can manage to provide both."

"Good." The emperor added, "This is a war I intend to win."

Vandover stood there until the extended silence

informed him he had been dismissed. He tried to leave without undue haste, but he was a busy man and he had duties to attend.

Denaro stood in the public lobby of the Walker compound, his tall and muscled frame filling the open space until Vandover felt as slight and insubstantial as a shadow. He showed his teeth in a cold smile. "Thank you for allowing me to see you."

The young man did not return the smile. "This is sanctuary, Minister," he responded in clipped tones. "I hope you don't mind being confined to the public lobby. We have privacy screens, however. If St. Colin were here, he'd see you in his apartments, but. . . ."

"Indeed." Vandover gathered his robes and seated himself behind a screen. Denaro hesitated, then joined him. The young man did not sit in a chair, he conquered it, and Vandover watched him appraisingly. This was a man Storm had trained for battle armor at Colin's behest, temporarily shielding him from Pepys' wrath. Now Denaro was out from behind Colin's protection and as the strongest contender to follow in the older man's footsteps, his own visibility was his protection. But it would not do to forget that Denaro wore armor . . . or that Storm had been his commander. He dampened his lips before offering, "I've come to see if there's anything I can do for you in Colin's absence."

Denaro's hand tightened on the arm of the chair, white knuckle lines stark against his tanned skin. But his face remained calm as he answered, "Removing our protective guard would be considerate. The compound stinks of Thraks."

"The Knights are here for your safety."

"Those aren't Knights."

"The emperor will be informed." Nothing would be done and the two of them knew it. Colin had had similar objections. If Pepys would not budge for Colin, he most certainly would not for Denaro.

"Thank you for your concern, Minister. Now, if you'll excuse me, there is much I need to do."

Vandover stood, relishing towering over the man still seated. "I understand, of course. Perhaps when Jonathan is more fully recovered, he can return to his duties as Colin's aide, even though Colin has not returned."

Denaro lost all color in his face. His jawline slacked. "What do you mean?"

Vandover feigned confusion. "Why ... surely you were told ... Jonathan was picked up several weeks ago and brought in by one of our Talons. He's comatose and Pepys has made him as comfortable as possible in the palace hospital wing. I'm sorry, Denaro. I thought you had been made aware of this."

The Walker got to his feet. The color which had drained from his face now returned in a blaze across his cheeks. Jonathan had been with Colin. They were both well aware of that and now Denaro was also aware that Pepys had been concealing vital information from him. "I'd like to request permission to see him."

Vandover shrugged. "It would do you little good. He appears to be in some sort of catatonic shock. He has the best of care, of course, and there is hope he will return to us. He is our best way of tracing Colin's whereabouts."

"Has Storm seen him yet?"

"The commander is a cautious and thorough man. Although I'm certain Jonathan will become one of his priorities, he has other concerns on his mind right now."

Denaro paused, apparently taking stock of what he knew. "There can be pressure brought to bear."

Vandover flicked dust motes off the sleeve of his robes. "Pepys is not disposed to tolerating any more civil disobedience," he answerly slowly. "Storm knows that Jonathan is readily available. After all, a comatose man is not likely to be going anywhere, is he? There are advantages to be taken of the vast Walker empire while there is still confusion over Colin's disappearance." He lowered his voice. "Storm wants Pepys off the Triad Throne. That is no longer any secret. To do so, he'll need . . . backing. He has gone to the Green Shirts. Now he will come to the Walkers. It's to his advantage to let Colin remain missing while he consolidates his position with you before he plays hero."

Denaro let his breath out with a hiss. He looked past Vandover, across the Walker lobby, then his gaze flicked back. "You know this."

"I am Minister of War. What would I be without intelligence sources? But Pepys is my emperor and no matter how badly he needs Jack Storm, I would not hesitate to let him know he uses a dangerous and ambitious tool."

"Nor would I," the young man echoed. He set his jaw. "Thank you, Baadluster, for taking me into your confidence."

Vandover edged out from the screened area. "You are most welcome," he answered. He bowed and left, aware that Denaro's intense gaze burned into him like a brand. As the Thraks guard let him through, Vandover allowed himself a small smile of triumph.

Jack stood by the bedside—more of a crèche, really, to support the patient's functions—and thought that Amber had not exaggerated. The man lying before him was only a shell of the person he'd known as Jonathan. Vigorous, immense, yet gentle as if afraid of his own strength—all that had been bled away from him. The underlying hiss and suck and hum of the equipment that kept him alive permeated the room.

Amber stirred at Jack's elbow. He sensed her withdrawing to the entrance of the room. He looked back. "Was he this bad when they found him?"

Her face was pale, expression drawn, as if the time they'd shared together had never happened. She nodded in answer to his question. "Nearly this bad. They got him on life support as quickly as they could. And then, he just declined."

He swept his gaze over the monitors, reading the obscure displays. It was obvious even to him that Jonathan clung to life by the faintest of grips. He raised his voice. "Observation?"

"Yes, sir," the near wall answered him. Whether the doctors beyond were flesh or mechanical, Jack could not tell.

"What are his chances?"

"He can be sustained indefinitely, but whether it is worth it to do so. . . ." the voice trailed off and

Jack knew he spoke to flesh. Only flesh worried about the quality of life. Machines worried only about function, on or off.

Jack looked back to Amber who stood braced by the door, her palms behind her slender hips and pressed to the wall. "Did he put up a fight before?"

She shook her head. "Jack, I don't know. Why?"

"I'm wondering if Colin was taken . . . or if he left voluntarily."

She straightened indignantly. "Colin wouldn't have left Jonathan like this!"

"Not wouldn't have, Amber—the proof is that he did leave him. I only wonder if he was forced to, or if he left on his own."

"How can you ask such a thing?"

Jack looked at her mildly. "I can ask because I'll need to know. Who found them? Did Colin take them to some faraway meeting place where he met more than he counted on? Or were they intercepted? Am I to start looking among friends or foes?"

She came toward him then. "I'm sorry. I thought—"

The corner of his mouth drew up. "Jonathan was my friend, too." He turned back to the crèche, sighing barely audibly. "What could you tell us, if you were able. . . ." Jack brushed his palm lightly over the man's limp arm, feeling the feverish dry texture of the other's skin.

The curls of Jonathan's thick dark hair stirred, as if attracted by some electricity between his head and Jack's hand. The Walker aide was pelted as thickly as some bear. He lay beneath the sterile sheets, his shoulders bared and the hair upon them was as thick as that upon his head. Jack dropped his hand upon the massive forearm—muscular potential, strong but not bulked. If he had been the type to wear a battle suit, he'd have been a behemoth.

At the touch of skin to skin, the near lifeless form convulsed. Amber's gasp echoed the clarion sound of alarms going off. Jack sprang back a step from the hospital bed as monitor screens danced with bright illumination.

"What's happening?" Amber called out, the edge of her voice thin and high with fear.

Jonathan's bulk jumped and thumped upon the bed. His convulsions began breaking and discharging leads and wires by the handful. Jack could hear sudden activity behind the observation wall and knew that help was on its way. Until then, to keep Jonathan's body from flopping off the bed, he reached out and held him down.

Time seemed to become thick and he stuck in it. He could hear Amber's voice, but not the words she said. They were too long and drawn out for him to make sense of them. She's panicky, he thought, and wondered at that, knowing that there were few things beyond her control and thought again that that must be the cause of her panic. He could not feel the unleashed energy of the life support crèche surging through himself as well as Jonathan's flailing body. He could not hear the crackle of the discharge nor sense his hair standing upon end as it did so. He knew only that Jonathan's hands were gripping him, dragging him down, pulling him close, and that the aide's eyes, ringed with white, were wide open. His mouth worked. "Help me," the sick man gasped, just before the hospital staff tore him from Jack's arms.

"A hypnotic induced coma," Baadluster said, his fleshy lips thinning in satisfaction. "Though a poorly constructed one. Jonathan might have died."

"Self-induced?"

The Minister of War shrugged, his storm crow robes moving sluggishly about his tall and lumpy form. "Perhaps. He's not said, and the staff tells me he's resting now. You heard more from him than anyone."

Jack frowned, remembering the frantic burbling of words that had spilled from Jonathan before the staff had managed to separate the two of them. He shook his head. "He was incoherent."

"I see," the minister said, but there was disbelief in his voice. "And you?" He looked to Amber. "Perhaps you caught something in all the confusion."

"Me?" Her face was still wan, and purple shadows dappled the hollows beneath her golden-brown eyes. "I thought he was dying."

Vandover paused. Then, "And that upset you, milady? But surely, in your time in under-Malthen, you've seen many a death."

She shot him a glare, but Jack stepped between them. Jack was tall, even among a battalion of big men who wore the battle armor. Vandover had to look up to meet his eyes.

Very quietly, Storm said, "You are Minister of War, Baadluster, but I think I need to remind you to be very, very careful who you battle with. The emperor has need of our services and your . . . discretion.''

Vandover's thick lips pursed without sound, but he withdrew to the doorway and stopped there. If he had paled, it could not be seen, for his complexion was always pasty. "The emperor sent me down with word that this latest development has pleased him, and he will see you tomorrow morning before your . . . procedure. In the meantime, both of us warn you that your freedom and safety is limited to this wing.'' He nodded abruptly. "Good evening, Commander Storm and Milady Amber.''

Amber shuddered, as if throwing off Vandover's scent. She looked through the observation wall at Jonathan's still form, now resting quietly. "He was keyed to you,'' she said.

"I know. What if he hadn't been found or. . . .'' Jack let his voice trail off. "I don't think Colin left him voluntarily. He wouldn't leave Jonathan to chance like that.'' He looked at her then, smiling. "We're going to disappoint Vandover.''

"Oh?''

"I presume you can get me out of here.''

She leaned into him. "Of course. Where to?''

"The only thing that Jonathan said that made any sense to me was Colin's meditation chamber. Jonathan mentioned it three times. Somewhere, in his scrambled memory, it's important.'' He dropped his arm about her shoulders.

"Then we'll get there.''

The Walker saint's apartments resonated with his personality. The rooms were both austere and rich . . . rich with the simple things of the worlds

Colin had touched. Jack stepped into them and wiped his hands down, his palms damp with the effort of breaking into the Walker complex without alerting either Thrakian guards or Walker staff. As the coolness of the empty rooms swept over him and he looked around he thought that he had never, in his recollection, had a place to call his own. As long as he could think back, he'd been housed in temporary places or barracks.

Amber sat gracefully on the redwood burl coffee table that had been one of Colin's favorite possessions. The three of them had held many a conference over it. "I've never been in the meditation chamber," she said.

"Ummm." Jack walked around the main room, eyeing artwork and office work, noting the clean yet not too orderly status of both, as if the occupant had just stepped out for a moment and would be back any second. "He planned on coming back," he said.

"I can tell." She rubbed her forearms. "Or he didn't have time to prepare."

Jack paused at the archway to the meditation chamber where a small flight of stairs led up. He looked over his shoulder. "Coming?"

"N–no. I don't think so."

He gave her a quick smile. "All right." He mounted the stairs and disappeared from her sight.

Events in her life since she'd met Jack had all but purged her of her psychic abilities—either purged her or walled them away so well she need never worry about them again—save for moments now and then when they prickled at her like St. Elmo's fire, an invisible dancer upon her nerves.

She chafed at her forearms now, as though trying to touch tattoos a shaman had once etched on her, gone now but not forgotten. She could feel the pull of Jack's presence on her like the tug of a golden rope.

Amber shifted her weight uneasily and looked about the room. She could sense Colin's presence as if it were a perfume lingering. Unconsciously, she took a deep breath, savoring it.

The meditation chamber stood half open, as if waiting for him. Jack hesitated before entering, taking a quick and practiced glance about, an action drilled into him by association with surveillance-shy Amber. He saw nothing overt, ducked his head and stepped over the threshold.

The chamber had been left set on display, for the moment he broached the field, gentle holo images came on, and he was surrounded by the worlds that man had touched since his intrusion into space. Jack never made it to the low, carved chaise longue of wood in the chamber's center where one might sit or lie down. Imprisoned by the orbit of worlds he had known, he stood, one hand half held upward as if to touch them . . . worlds as they'd been before sand or war or even man. Spinning almost into his grasp and then away were Dorman's Stand, Opus, Malthen and then . . . his throat constricted.

It spilled through his fingers like the illusion it was: verdant Claron, whose untouched wildernesses had once given him back his sanity. Jack curled his fingers, unable to hold the image of the planet that was now a firestormed bit of char undergoing the painstaking process of terraforming and rebirth.

He had done that much, at least. Unable to save his home world of Dorman's Stand or the others from Thrakian *sand*, at least he had been able to start the restoration of Claron. It had been flamed to scourge the first traces of *sand* away . . . and to remove him.

The display operating was a long one. He finally realized he should move and retired to the bench where Colin would have sat to watch and think. He watched until it came to him that he wasn't seeing what was in front of him, that he'd retreated into a near trance, his eyes no longer focusing. The sand planet Milos swirled past along with bitter memories. Jack blinked. He stood up in defeat.

"Jack . . . are you all right?"

Amber had been calling him. He raised his voice. "Be right down. I haven't found anything."

The display stopped the moment he stepped out of the sensor field. Jack stopped and looked back. Milos hung at the edge of his peripheral vision, fading away into nothingness. It was the site of his most bitter defeat, but he felt a catch in his throat as he lost it once again, before he went down to join Amber.

Chapter 4

Alarms shattered the night. Amber rolled from Jack's side to her feet, shaking her head to scatter the last of sleep, even as she cursed the interruption of their rest. Jack sat up.

"What is it?"

He listened, picking up security code signals in the alarm and gave a grunt as he bent to pull on his boots. They'd both slept clothed, uneasy under the protection of Pepys. "Not the emperor's wing. It's right here—with us."

Her brown eyes with their golden flecks widened. "Nobody's bothering us. . . ."

"Jonathan!"

Storm made the door first, but she was right on his heels.

The breach in the wing that had set off the alarm gaped before them—rank, scoured, and still smoking.

"My God," Amber said, as she slowed. "They blasted their way through."

"Stay back."

She halted behind his warning hand. "Why?"

"That was done by a suit."

Her response was drowned out by the rattle of Thrakian carapaces on the corridor floor. Instead of talking, she grabbed Jack's restraining hand but he shook her off.

"Thraks!"

"Answering the alarm. They're part of the guard now. They'll be here as soon as they seal off the wing." Even as he spoke, Jack moved forward into the blasted outer lab that had surrounded Jonathan's hospital room. Amber followed close behind.

In the shadowy interior, machinery sputtered and sparked. Plastic and metal crunched under his steps. Amber had not pulled on her boots. Biting her lip, she halted, unable to go farther, but past Jack's frame she could see a tall and darker shadow pulling at leads and machinery with quick, effective rips, freeing Jonathan's limp body.

"Drop him, Denaro," Jack said quietly.

The battle armored man turned, the massive Jonathan cradled in one plated arm as though the size of a child. The visor was down, screen darkened.

"He's mine. You bastards have had him long enough. If you want him, come take him."

Amber's breath hissed inward. By that faint sound, Jack placed her location as well behind him and out of the wreckage of the room, and the tension in his shoulders relaxed just a bit. The plastic and glass shards littering the floor kept her out of harm's way.

His answer was to move against Denaro, fast, quick, unpredictable—the only advantage flesh had against battle armor. He'd trained Denaro— the man had been one of the Knights' best before he'd gone rogue. Denaro had always been St. Colin's man, not a soldier of the Triad Throne, and

Jack had known it when he took him in. And just as he knew who was in the armor, he knew how Denaro would react to a frontal attack.

Amber screamed then, as if realizing what she saw.

Gauntlet fire turned the dark air orange. Jack tumbled past it, just out of range, feeling the heat of it whistle by. At Denaro's feet, he crouched, grasped a dagger of jagged glass and stabbed upward, toward a chink in the Flexalink coverage, not where the back of the knee was, but where he knew it would be as Denaro power vaulted to avoid his attack.

The dagger skittered in his hand, made a screeing noise as it connected, then slipped inward. It was torn out of his grasp as the jump carried Denaro away. Jack immediately twisted backward, but he was too late, betrayed by his own body, as the other kicked out.

The heavy boot caught him a glancing blow to the chest—but even an angled blow from a suit was enough to drive him across the room where a wall stopped him the hard way. Jack let himself slide downward, forcing muscles that were convulsed in pain to relax.

Denaro came to ground, and set Jonathan aside. "Don't do this, Commander," he said. There was an edge of pain in his voice. He reached down and pulled the glass dagger out, its edges crimson.

Jack rolled over into a ball, legs under him, gathering himself. He looked up and met the charcoal screen of the visor, knowing a human gaze lay behind it.

"I can't let you do this."

"You can't stop me. I'm suited and you—you're not."

"That's where you're wrong. If you'd stayed in the Knights long enough, you'd have learned your weaknesses."

The gauntlet fired, but Jack had leapt already, inside and under it. Jonathan's flaccid bulk protected him from a second spray.

"I thought," Denaro said, and an aggrieved pant interrupted his words, "I thought you knew who the real enemy was."

"Never doubt it," Jack answered, just as he launched himself, and Amber screamed, "Don't shoot!"

He never knew if she'd meant it for Denaro, or for the hard-bodied aliens that suddenly filled the ruined lab and room. The reek of their excitement filled his nostrils even as the beam caught him twisting and brought him down. The warrior Thraks smelled like hot brass and he hated it worse than the smell of death which washed over him as the floor caught him up with ungentle force.

Amber shrilled, "Stop it! You'll kill them both!"

Denaro leaned over Jack. He picked him up by the nape of his neck, his gauntlet still warm and stinking. In the other arm, he carried Jonathan and the Walker aide's slack face stared unseeingly.

"Leave him," Storm got out. The side of his face was numb, and he tasted the sweet flat iron of his own blood. "Pepys brought me back to find Colin. I swear to you I'm going after him."

The visor showed him a blurred reflection of himself, but it was Denaro who answered, "Too late. We've waited too long." The armor shuddered and the room shifted. Jack realized he was being carried along, dangling by his neck as Denaro used him as a shield. "You should not have tried to stop me."

"Try, hell!" Jack twisted in the gauntlet and brought his boot heels up to the neck joint with a snap that forced the helmeted head back. Another snap and the seam began to give way.

Amber put her hands to her mouth, watching Jack retaliate. If there was a man alive who could fight a suit bare-handed, he was that man. But already he'd paid a price too dear. She heard the Flexalinks sing in protest as he kicked up, not once but twice. Denaro rocked back and staggered through the massive hole in the outside wall.

The Thraks could wait no longer. Their quarry was bolting. Even as Jack found the vital weak spot in the helmet to suit seal, they swarmed.

Her throat went raw as she shouted them off. Jack slipped to the floor where he lay, crimson and blistered with laser fire, and the battle armor beat off a last attacker before turning and running, powering out of her sight with a speed she would not have believed except that she knew the suits and what they could do.

A second later, K'rok was there, the massive and furry Milot overwhelming her as he buffeted the Thraks into submission with his bellows. Sarge was there, too, calling for live medics.

Numbly, she stepped aside from the Guard. They'd never catch Denaro. She shoved aside a Thraks standing wobbling on one chitined leg, not caring that he crashed to the floor with a clacking and hissing as she went to Jack.

There was blood everywhere. The air stank of it and Jack's hand was slippery with it when she grasped it. The flesh she pressed was chill and passive and she looked quickly to see if Jack was still conscious. His eyes flickered and he moaned as the medics reached them and lifted his body off the shattered flooring onto a gurney.

His gaze met hers, but she could see he was having difficulty focusing. She leaned close as the medics locked the gurney into position and began wheeling it toward the operating lab.

His breath tickled her ear. "Get . . . the observation tape."

"I will, but why—"

"Get the tape before . . . Baadluster. It wasn't necessary . . ." Jack took a shallow, wheezing breath. "It wasn't necessary for Denaro to take Jonathan. He did . . . to make sure I'd follow. The tape will tell me . . . where. Fair fight . . . Thraks did the worse damage." With a trembling effort, he closed his fingers over her hand. "Understand? Nothing's going to stop us now."

"Yes." Amber loped now, to keep pace with the gurney and the medics, unable to bend close enough to talk with Jack. The lab doors opened and the medics tore Jack's hand away from her. She stood for long minutes as the doors shut in front of her, cradling her right hand until long after Jack's blood dried on her skin.

Then she realized Jack had given her something to do, and she hurried to take care of it before someone else beat her to the tape. It was nothing to get the tape . . . it took a few minutes to rig the system as though it had malfuctioned or perhaps Denaro had tampered with it to explain the absence of any recording on the blank tape she substituted.

Seeing him in the healing crèche was little better than being left outside the operating bay. Sealed off, all she could see was his face. The rest of him was swaddled in medical equipment and a reconstruction matrix. A bright flush of fever mottled an otherwise too pale complexion. There was no rise and fall of his chest from breathing, under the matrix and in cold sleep, there could be none. Vandover shadowed her, but she refused to let his presence warn her off. *He could be dead*, she thought uneasily, *and the bastard's enjoying watching me wait.*

Vandover dropped a hand to her shoulder. She squelched the flinch of reaction.

"Because of his injuries," the man in black said softly, "he'll be under for two weeks instead of several days. The doctors asked me to tell you."

Baadluster was used to being the bearer of bad news. She could tell this revelation did not particularly distress him.

"Whatever it takes," Amber said tonelessly. He stood beside her a few moments longer, then withdrew and went about his imperial business. She waited until she was certain he was gone before she let the tears brimming in her eyes fall upon her face. She wished she could share Jack's triumph, but Vandover's continued presence set off the alarms of her faded intuition. The mind-loop was out of her hands and in those

of their uneasy allies. Jack had not worried—
but she did.

She worried that whatever chance Jack'd had to
go through imprint and come back the man she
loved grew slimmer by the day.

Chapter 5

He was whole again. Young and eager, though the core of him was ice as if he were chilled down—but he couldn't be, he had never been, and the army wouldn't risk cold sleep on a raw recruit . . . too expensive. He'd gotten here on his own hook, and now he was here, and in, with a spindly, pot-bellied NCO bellowing at him—

"No suit, no soldier! If you hear it once, you'll hear it a thousand times. Those of you who made it through Basic to get to us—you ain't done yet! We're going to winnow you again because only the best get to wear armor and you don't look like the best to me. Do you?"

"NO, SIR!"

"But if I make you the best, and the ones of you who make it through my camp *are* the best, and I do it not because I like you but because *it is my job to give the best to the Knights*, then you'll be good enough to wear the armor. And if you're good enough to wear the armor, then you'll know you're the best because there isn't anybody else on God's green lands good enough to tell you you're the best! Your ass is going to depend on that suit once you earn it. I'm going to teach you how to wear it, use it, eat, sleep, and shit in it, and repair it. You will treat nothing as well as you treat your armor, not even your mother! Do you understand, boys?"

"YES, SIR!"

His mother. Jack caught a glimpse of memory, of his brown-haired, freckle-dusted, sad-eyed mother, looking across a field of shadow and sun toward him, waving good-bye . . . and he remembered. He won the armor and lost Milos . . . and the Thraks devoured his own planet as they had half a dozen others, and her bones undoubtedly lay covered by Thrakian *dust*, unmourned until now.

He would have cried, but he was too cold to cry and the tears would have frozen anyway.

Pepys looked up briefly from his web of com links, his red hair drifting in its own cloud of electricity. He damped down the transmit as Vandover shifted impatiently, waiting to claim his attention. "What is it?"

"The lab says Storm will be coming out of imprint shortly."

"So soon?"

Baadluster controlled his emotions by fisting his hands, nails digging into his sweaty and itchy palms. "It's been twelve days."

The emperor leaned back in his chair. He was slight and, as he aged, was becoming wizened. The yellow-white sun of Malthen never tanned but always freckled him, in the garish way given to some redheads, and his emerald eyes contrasted sharply with his complexion as his stare pinioned Vandover. "And what will we have when he reemerges? Will we have a tool we can use?"

He inclined his head. He would have given his

soul to hear the flow of communications Pepys controlled—to be able to manipulate the worlds of the Triad Throne and even the free and far-flung worlds of the Dominion simply through the networks Pepys held contracts on. No communication occurred that did not pass through the filter of the Triad Throne. Emperor Regis, who ruled before Pepys, had been good at wielding these reins, but Pepys was incredible. Vandover contained his fervor. "You will have a loyal fighting machine."

"Will I? One hopes. And what of Amber?"

"She holds vigil." Vandover's face hardened in an expression his emperor could not help but catch—and interpret. The words were forced through pasty-white lips which slowly regained a more natural color.

"There," Pepys said quietly, abandoning his mocking tone, "is a woman, despite what you think of her." But he knew well, even better than Vandover himself, what the man thought of her. He paused, listening to something coming in, his thoughts momentarily abstracted. Then he looked back at Vandover.

"If it worked," he said, "we have saved my throne."

"May I suggest that we are finished with milady's value to us?"

"We need her as long as I need Jack."

"You can tell him you have sent Amber elsewhere. Malthen is, for all purposes, in a state of siege. We have troops keeping the agra lanes open for food transport. Otherwise, the Walkers are doing a good job of pressuring us."

Pepys blinked, a predatory hooding of his brilliant eyes. "I would not believe us if I were Jack."

"You're his emperor."

"A free man has no emperor. Amber may be the only hostage we have to keep Storm in line." Pepys stroked one of the fiber leads in his com net. "She's yours, Vandover—but only after Jack is off-planet. Whatever you do with her, *I want nothing traced back to either of us.* Understood?"

Vandover fought to contain the fierce heat lancing him. "A wise decision. She is, after all, a common criminal."

"Common is the last word I'd apply to her." The emperor shrugged. "Report to me when he's awakened." He spun back to his console, listening once again, fingers tapping out judgments, decisions, and notes on the keypad balanced across one thigh.

Vandover bowed himself out of the room. He wondered what Jack Storm was remembering now.

Sand blighted the horizon. As Jack exited staging, a rust and beige swath of hell met his eyes wherever he looked. Equipment racks swayed in the hot summer wind. He let out a pungent curse and the Milot techs working on the repair line looked up, bestial faces wrinkling and looking away. Solder popped and he could smell the flush from armor on the far racks. Only the Milot working lead stayed at attention as Jack walked over.

"I know it's hot," he said to the massive alien. "But you've got to keep dust out of the circuitry. You're supposed to be under the domes." Canopy sheeting overhead snapped in the wind. Its shade striped across the Milot's face.

"Lieutenant," the Milot said, his voice rumbling from a cavernous chest. "If you want to take a patrol out today, we must be working wherever we can. Dust is the least of your problems." And the being waved a probe at the barren horizon where transport ships were supposed to be fielded.

"My concern," snapped Jack, "is the welfare of my men. I don't want to hear that the suits aren't being repaired properly or aren't fully powered up. I don't want to hear that any of your crew is siphoning off supplies."

The Milot grunted. His piglike gaze flicked away and returned. "And I suppose you be believing we grow berserkers out of your men, too. You'll have your rack ready when you are, Lieutenant." He spat into the dust at their feet. "And all you have to worry about will be *sand*."

In his sleep, memory comes together in a violent clash with dream. He remembers why it is he hates Thraks and *sand* and doesn't trust Milots. What it is like to fight long after the suits run low on power, and some of them grind to a halt, too heavy for a man to move on his own, leaving the wearers to die a horrible death, entombed in the battle armor. He tastes the bitter seeds of defeat again, abandoned by superior officers who have decided to cut their losses on Milos. He knows that his emperor, Regis, has been manipulated into this decision by his treacherous nephew Pepys, and that Regis will lose his throne and his life. But this is a nightmare from which he cannot awake. The transport ships will never arrive, except for a few. Recall will not be sounded. The Knights are among those troops deemed to be expendable. And even as he remembers, has the sum total of his life given back to him, childhood, family, adolescence, a shadow follows him. Like a snake of darkness, it swallows up his thoughts even as he's fully regained them, and he can never go backward, only forward into his mind.

Desperately, he tries to confront the snake which is devouring all that he has been given back. It is hot inside the armor, and his grid is blurred by his own sweat, and the various leads clipped to his torso are more than irritating, they have become painful. The chamois at his back absorbs the salt and water dripping down.

Thraks are attacking, yes, but that is memory and this attack from within—it is reality. He has been betrayed again.

As he reaches out with his thoughts, a spark arcs out. He is trapped by Thraks, his men are down, power going, abandoned to the *sand* and he feels the new life stirring at his back. It reaches out for him, a white blossoming fire that beats back the dark devouring snake.

Bogie. Bogie was alive with him, even then! And the realization repels Jack as he is caught within his mind, watching battle armor split like brittle eggshells, not to free his men, but to spit out immense saurian creatures, hatched from the helpless bodies of his men, frills spread in berserker frenzy, to attack both Knights and Thraks. The Milots, knowing they are losing their world, have indeed seeded the parasitic berserker lizards in whatever flesh they can. Barracks rumor has become nightmare reality.

And his own alien bonds flesh with him even as Jack fights to live.

The furious will to survive carries him through.

Gauntlet fire cuts down the Thraks, their carapaces popping and fizzing in the flame, and even his suit, too drained now to work efficiently, feels the heat. He has come full circle as the recall signal pulses across his com. He looks across a pit of Thrakian chiton and human flesh into a shadow, a blot of darkness across his visor and finally, stupidly, recognizes a transport.

They are being scraped off the surface of Milos like so many squashed bugs . . . all that is left of the Dominion's finest. He knows what battle fatigue is, and shock, and swims though it anyway, grabbing an arm strap from the transport hover, and stepping onto the running board as it lifts him from a pit of death—and he's the only one still up and moving. He waits impassively as the hover brings him cross-country to staging where, he can tell, evacuation is in an absolute rout.

A tech helps him peel off the suit, nose wrinkling at the smell and reek of his imprisonment. Sweat drips off him like a toxic wash. He kicks out of his boots and leaves the equipment, not looking back. The noise and turmoil of staging as they make ready to load three massive cold ships brings him back to reality sometime after the crew has checked his palm and retinal prints.

The cryo nurse puts a kit into his hand. "You'll need this, soldier. Showers are to the right. This is your locker number. Stow your kit in it before you report to the lab."

The man will not meet Jack's gaze. He says, although it is not necessary, and he knows the nurse has no time to listen. "We lost Milos."

"No kidding."

"I'm sorry. I tried."

The nurse pauses. Jack feels the impatience and weariness of the men lined up behind him. The nurse shrugs, answering, "You think you're responsible for the whole damn war? Now get a move on, soldier. We've got a deadline. We've got to get our asses out of here before the bugs know they've won."

Jack showers, luxuriating in the feel of real water, before the cut off leaves him half lathered and dripping. He towels off, dresses from the kit, general issue that fits much too tightly across the shoulders and thighs—general issue not being cut for a man who wears armor—and joins the masses in the hold as they stow their gear. Over the com lines, they receive a stream of instruction, the harsh voice falling, for the main part, on deaf ears. They are troops. They've been through this before. The only thing they want now is a hot meal—not possible before chill down—and some rest. The rest they'll get: months in cold sleep. The cold ship hold is immense and stacked to the ceiling with the coffinlike cryos. He works his way down the aisles to his locker and opens it.

The Flexalinks wink at him, an obscene pearl hanging from the equipment racks. The NCO loading the transport bellows once more, and this time he hears the announcement, "Your suits have been infested. They will be maintained in quarantine until we can determine their status and either flush or destroy them."

No suit, no soldier.

"Line up and file in, in an orderly fashion," the NCO bellows again, and around him, he can hear the tired shuffling of those still on their feet, the ones who are able enough to walk.

He tells himself he is lucky. He tells himself that thousands have died so a few hundred can make it to these transports. He tells himself that he will somehow bring victory out of this horrifying defeat. He is still a Knight, and he still wears battle armor.

The suit swings on its rack, splashed with soot and blood and the ichor of Thraks. It smells of Milos and war. It looks like a denizen of Hell. It is bonded inexorably with him.

Just as he begins to integrate his past with his present, the devourer strikes without mercy.

The eyelids of the frozen man begin to flicker.

Chapter 6

The coracle rocked violently as it was released, ejected like an empty shell into a decaying orbit. Bogie fine-tuned the armor's sensors to listen after the Ash-farel vessel. He abruptly damped them as a human scream cut like a laser across the frequency. Fear and pain vibrated through his system as he lay curled in the tiny rescue vehicle's equipment bay where, well-camouflaged, he had been overlooked by the aliens.

Pain and fear were not unknown to Bogie. He had carried Jack through many such ordeals. Now it resonated inside him uneasily until he understood the edge of the feeling: he, too, was afraid. The revelation was both heartening and disheartening. It meant he had evolved enough, was alive enough, to fear death. Now at last he understood some of Jack's hesitation to fight. Death was the dark side of war. And only a living being would fear death.

He had come far, but he did not cherish the feeling. He was a warrior, he knew that, he savored battle and victory. Now, in the echo of Colin's anguish, he knew he would never be the same.

He made plans to emerge when the Ash-farel mother ship pulled away. He would correct the coracle's orbit. He would wait for Jack, who would come as Colin had promised he would, and Bogie would then point the way as it was his duty to do. Until then, he would tap into the armor's power circuit and take the energy he needed to continue to live. He would try not to listen to the recording of St. Colin's capture.

It frightened him too much.

"I want," Vandover said to the computer screen, "someone disposed of in under-Malthen."

The image looking back at him showed no emotion, nor did he expect it to. The man's skin was sallow and his pupils too wide under the influence of *ratt*. "Who?" the man said.

"Never mind who. I'll give you a body . . . you make the arrangements."

"Ahhh." Illumination showed on the old man's face. "I'll need twenty-four hours' notice."

"Consider it given."

Wrinkles deepened momentarily in his contact's expression, then he shrugged. "I can handle it. What about the ident chip?"

Satisfaction broadened Vandover's smile. "She doesn't carry one," he said. "Do whatever you want."

"All right." The screen went dark as the com line closed.

With a little luck, Vandover reflected, Amber's body would never be identified properly—or even found. And if it was, all signs would point to another terrorist atrocity against Pepys by the Green Shirts. No, disposing of Amber was a strategy which would work well whatever its consequences.

He pushed away from the keyboard with long, tapering fingers that ached as if they could already feel the curve of her throat within their grasp.

A com light flickered, signaling another incoming call. Vandover hesitated. Pepys would be demanding his time and he still had field reports to evaluate . . . but anything coming in over this line would be from his own security units within the World Police or the local sweepers. A morsel of information from there was too sweet to ignore. He opened the line.

The screen stayed dark. The informant did not wish his face shown, then, but Vandover's grid confirmed the retinal pattern of the speaker and he knew immediately who talked to him.

"Minister?"

"I'm here," Vandover replied carefully. His screen did not relay such niceties of information to the other caller. Baadluster winced a little at hearing the harsh accent of under-Malthen mingled with a touch of the Outward Bound planets as the informant spoke again.

"Several years ago you were looking for . . . a custom weapon."

A chill thrilled its way up Vandover's spine. "A weapon?"

"Yes. Molded for a specific need. You went through Winton for its inception, but when he was killed, you lost track of that weapon."

"Ah," was all Vandover breathed in confirmation. This was unexpected serendipity, indeed. Then, "You've located it?"

"Yes and no. I have the weapon's identity. You'll have to go from there."

Vandover's knuckles whitened. Winton had died without passing on all of his information to his partner, even such vital information as this. Undoubtedly, the former security chief had been as uneasy in his alliance with Vandover as Vandover had been with Winton. A plan some fifteen years in the making had ground to a halt. He'd been unable to access Winton's secret files, but here, finally, was the data he needed. "All right," he said. "What do you want from me?"

The informant named a figure and added, "And passage off-planet."

"Done. How do I verify what you're going to tell me?"

There was a verbal shrug in the pause that followed. Then the informant said, "You know the subliminal programming. Trigger it. The assassinations should follow."

"Good enough. Who is my missing weapon?"

"A street hustler named Rolf had a stable of kids working for him. Usual scams. His contact with Winton was well-hidden. But the one you want is a girl called Amber. She's not on the street any more and she never carried a chip, but—"

"Never mind," Vandover answered coldly. "I know where to start looking. You'll find your money at the usual drop." He cut the call short and sat looking at the darkened screen.

All those years under his nose and he'd never even guessed. It made sense to him now why Winton had not had her eliminated, making Storm even more vulnerable. Winton had not known the targets or the programming, but Vandover didn't doubt he'd been trying to ferret the information out so that he could do the manipulation. Each of them had kept secret from the other a vital part of the plan, forcing them to work in tandem with one another, despite their differences.

Vandover stroked the keyboard lightly. "Winton, my boy, you were clever." The hit on Amber would have to be canceled. Or perhaps not. A postponement would suit as well. She was much more subdued since the evacuation of Bythia. He would give his right arm to know what had happened on that fringe planet, how Winton's plans had gone awry and gotten him killed instead of reaching fruition. Perhaps she was no longer the weapon she had been groomed to be. He had never sensed any psychic fires banked within her, yet Winton had assured him the assassin being groomed for them was a genuine talent, unlike those charlatans Pepys kept bottled up in the east wing. So genuine a talent that the strike could be directly to the heart or the brain . . . swift, unstoppable, and virtually undetectable.

He must investigate the information carefully before acting. A good place to start would be the powerful loan maker, Sadie, who'd given the girl safe harbor more than once. Sadie would cooperate. She was a businesswoman skilled in the art of compromise, a reed that would bend in the wind rather than be broken.

Vandover placed a call. He would stay the inevitable, but it would be only a delay. If the girl proved false or useless to him anyway, she would still have to be removed.

Chapter 7

Amber was dozing, forehead to her knees, folded up in the corridor like a chair someone had tossed carelessly aside. The rank scent of Thraks wafted over her and she heard their constant clicking become agitated chatter through her half-dreams. Doors opened and the sounds awakened her fully.

She had lifted her head, wincing as a neck muscle kinked. She had done vigils in worse places by far, on concrete and permaplast streets without soul or hope, in backwater holes with murderers skulking about, on faraway worlds where, even surrounded by friends, the agony of waiting for Jack to return was almost too much to bear.

But this morning's vigil had worn her out in a way no other had, and as she met the stare of the nurse standing across the corridor, she gleaned no comfort from the man's words.

"He's out of it. A couple of hours on dialysis and we'll be able to let visitors in."

Amber got to her feet, slender legs unfolding to hold her, unaware of the technician's masculine reaction to her grace. She carefully rubbed the sleep from one eye. "How is he?"

"A little disoriented. We put a piggyback on his

tape to bring him up to date—it's been twenty-
seven years since that imprint was made."

Weariness fled. "You did what?"

The nurse looked over his shoulder. His bulk
blocked the lab door very effectively, and he listened to something happening behind him, before
he looked back to her. His jaw set. "We added on
a short orientation tape."

"I know what you meant. Who the hell author-
ized that?"

"Pepys," the nurse said. With that, he backed
up and the door slid shut. Hard glittering eyes
watched her until the barrier sealed them off.

"*Shit,*" Amber muttered, and clenched one fist.
The Thraks in the corridor came to attention, their
facial masks pulling into Kabuki contortions of
expression. Jack had once taught her how to read
them and she now saw aggression and command.
"Don't worry, boys," she said aloud, wondering
what Pepys had done. "But I suggest, for your own
good, there be a changing of the guard before Jack
comes out of that lab. He doesn't like Thraks."
With a tight smile, she turned and left. There were
things to do before she could end her vigil.

The Thraks had been replaced by an honor
guard of Knights when she returned. She eyed
them as she entered the medical wing corridor,
her attention caught by their gleaming armor of
many different colors. Jack's own white armor
was so white it was iridescent even though it had
been damaged over the years. A sudden sense of
loss hit her, and she felt a fluttering inside her
throat, a panicky, tickling surge as she wondered
if it or Colin could ever be found.

The guard parted, exposing Vandover Baadluster. He had given up his somber black robes for those of charcoal . . . a slight, psychological change and one which she pondered as he inclined his head to her.

"Milady Amber."

"Minister," she answered. Triumph flooded her abruptly and, though she felt her face warm with its intensity, she savored it. She had managed to deal with him without Jack's presence, but the knowledge that Jack would soon be able to back her up made her stronger.

Vandover's flat eyes glinted slightly as if guessing her emotion and her triumph turned swiftly to anger. Anger she could deal with. She let her words stay in her throat. She would not lose her advantage by throwing it away.

"We've been waiting," Vandover said. "I was most surprised to arrive here and find you missing. But then, the nurse told me he had spoken with you. You look well."

Amber put her chin up. She was tall, but the Minister of War was taller. "Thank you. When can I see him?"

"Now . . . if you're ready."

She hesitated. Thoughts flooded her, too many to pin down. Jack had his victory, at last. What would it mean to him? To them? Where was he now? Why wasn't he striding out to meet her?

"Milady?" Vandover prompted softly.

"Of course." She stepped through the aisle formed by the honor guard, followed by Baadluster, the fabric of his long overtunic whispering with his lumbering gait. She barely heard the noise, yet it brought a sense of foreboding as though a legion whispered evil of Pepys' minister. *An omen*, she thought as they entered the interior lab, *and one which I don't need.*

He sat with his back to them, wearing a clean white jumpsuit which echoed the pallor of his convalescence. She crossed the portal and came to a hesitant stop, aware that she barred Baadluster and the others from entering the lab behind her. He heard them nevertheless. He put up his right hand, four-fingered, snapped off the console deck, and removed his ear set. She saw then that he'd been listening to something.

Before he even swiveled in the chair, she knew. There were lines of tension across that familiar back. Tension and apprehension. And when he turned to face her, there was a pleasant blankness across his plain, high cheekboned face and in his light blue eyes. For a moment, her heart stuttered in her chest—but then she saw the same keen intelligence in his eyes that he'd always had and knew he'd at least retained that much.

As he stood, his eyes spoke before the man did. *Who are you?*

Her knees turned to water. One shoulder touched the portal framing, bracing her, as she listed slightly. Her ears buzzed.

"You must be Amber," he said, reaching for her.

She slapped his hand away. "I'm fine." Shivering, she pulled herself upright again and let Baadluster brush past her.

The minister gave Jack a masculine hug. "Let me welcome you back, my boy."

Amber watched Jack's faintly puzzled expression over the top of Baadluster's shoulder. Vandover released him. "Back after twenty some years of exile, one of the emperor's finest."

"Only to find a new emperor and the same enemy," Jack responded. There was very little warmth in his voice. "Though I understand we've become allies. I'm ready for debriefing when you are."

"Good. Emperor Pepys would like to see you as soon as possible."

"I understand." He caught Amber's gaze for a moment, then looked about him where two techs were still charting monitors. She became aware that leads still attached him to the lab console. "I'll be ready in about an hour as soon as the techs are convinced my blood sugar's stabilized and there's no hypothermia."

"Done." Baadluster signaled the guard, and they about faced and left.

Amber stayed. She ignored the observation monitors as she stepped closer and shivered at the stranger's expression in the eyes of her lover. Damn him, he made her break all her rules! "Don't do this to me," she told him. "I don't care what the advantage is. You're playing right into their hands. They added an imprint of their own onto your mind loop. God knows what they've programmed into you."

Anger flashed in his eyes. "God doesn't have to know," he said quietly. "I do. I can't tell you what you want me to say. I don't know you anymore—"

His name wrenched out of her, leaving her throat clenched in pain.

His face paled. "I'm sorry," he said. "I really am. They tell me I'm supposed to go retrieve the head of the Walker sect. I've got a lot to get ready. If you'll excuse me. . . ."

"Then you're still going after Colin?"

"I'm a soldier. This is my assignment. I don't have any choice."

"No," she said, and turned away blindly, unable to face him any longer. "And neither do I." She bolted from the lab and knew he would not call her back.

Vandover Baadluster snared her at the corridor's bend. His hand came out and caught her wrist. He blocked her instinctive kick and she stood, breathing hard. She strained at his hold, then paused, wild-eyed, at his restraint.

"Leave me," she said, voice low and deadly.

"Regardless of what you think and feel, *I* am not responsible for what happened to Jack Storm."

"You killed him!"

"Someone did, yes, I think we agree on that. But Pepys has other hands that do his dirty work from time to time." Baadluster's pasty face took on a glow. "It's not in my scheme of things to have Storm decommissioned just when we need his peculiar talent most."

She noticed then that there were no Thraks or other Knights about. The minister had had the wing cleared. She stilled in his grip. "What do you want from me?"

"I think it safe to say I want the same thing you want: not to send a reborn, *innocent* man out into a maelstrom of difficulties and war that he is only half aware of."

"And how do you propose to cure the situation?"

Baadluster smiled, his thick lips compressing. "I suggest we send you with him, dear Amber, to guard his back."

"I'd sooner ally with a Milot berserker than conspire with you."

His eyebrows arched and his icy fingers tightened about her wrist. She fought to keep back a cry of pain.

"Don't play with me, milady. I do not hold a high opinion of you."

"Nor I you."

"Then," and his voice lowered, "we understand each other. We each have motives of our own. I offer you this: Madam Sadie kept a mind-loop of you. My sources tell me that your traumatic stay on Bythia leached away many of your . . . shall we call them skills? You'll need them back if you want to be of any help to Jack. Your imprint can be done quickly. Do you agree?"

Amber's thoughts tumbled. Unsuccessfully, she tried to center them. To be re-imprinted as an assassin—to have her psychic channels opened back up—to once again have subliminal programming within her that she could not control . . . she'd gone through hell to have that taken from her once. Why would she willingly ask that it be done to her a second time?

To help Jack, that's why.

And she also knew there was no way Vandover could know the extent of what he was offering her. He might guess at the coldblooded skills of an adept street fighter but there was no way he could know the rest of her secrets. None. She could con-

trol her killer instinct this time. And there was no
one alive who could trigger her subliminal programming, her list of targets.

She smiled hesitantly. "All right. We're agreed."

Baadluster's hard, dark eyes glittered. "Good,"
he said. He released her wrist and then, astonish-
ingly, brought his hand up and stroked her tawny
mane of hair once, caressingly. "Good," he repeated.

Chapter 8

He watched the young woman leave, trailing per-
fumed anger in her wake. She stirred dreams in
him, but he did not know her, not really. Jack
turned back to the lab console, retrieved the disk
that he'd been listening to and slipped it into a
pocket. The thoughts on that disk, like the body
he'd awakened to, were those of a stranger. He
was older, without having remembered living it,
scarred without knowing whose battles he'd
fought, loved without understanding how to return it.

Not that he was an old man, not by any means—
he guessed his age to be in the late twenties to
early thirties range though his linear age was
closer to his mid-fifties. And he had healed well,
though skin stretched a little gingerly over his ribs
and there was a knot or two there which ached.
But he had been left with the feeling, since awakening that morning, that he was wearing someone
else's skin, someone who had loyalties and loves
he could not begin to comprehend.

The disk, sketchy at best, had confirmed as
much. He apologized mentally to the other Jack
Storm for usurping his life. There was nothing he
could do about it now. The disk had not given him

memories but warnings, dire warnings to help keep him alive if the worst should happen. Once again, Jack Storm was a man with but half a life— now he was missing the end instead of the beginning.

"Commander Storm?" The nurse technician leaned into the otherwise empty lab. "We're done monitoring you. I'm told the emperor wants to see you as soon as possible."

He nodded. Thanks to the disk, he had a fairly good idea who his enemies were this time around and Pepys was high on the list.

Amber shivered despite herself. She shut her jaw firmly and clenched her teeth, determined not to give Vandover the satisfaction of knowing that cold sleep daunted her. But to sleep the sleep of near-death in the arms of enemies was a far different prospect than doing it in the embrace of friends.

The Minister of War brushed shoulders with her. She recoiled from the contact, but he seemed not to notice as the taxi bumped to a halt, its hovers whining. He dropped a cassette into her hand.

She closed her hand over it without looking. "No unexpected surprises?"

"You'll find Madam Sadie's seal on it."

Amber dropped the cassette into a hip pocket. Sadie had once been an unflappable friend. Now a traitor. She did not find the information assuring.

"Do you wish me to accompany you?"

"No."

The minister did not look surprised. "Very well. I'll be back for you tomorrow." Unspoken was the warning for her to be here, awaiting him. Amber did not rise to the bait. She would be waiting. For now, she had nowhere else to go.

Pepys was waiting in the audience hall. It was empty, banners slack upon their rods in the domed ceiling, daises empty, he sitting almost forlornly in a chair to one side. Jack recognized him only because he'd been shown photos of him. Yet as he approached, a familiarity prickled him like pins and needles. Yes, he'd known the frizzy red hair would drift finely about the man's head as if filled with static electricity. And he'd expected the hard green gaze of the imperial eyes.

He approached the man in the chair, came to a halt, and saluted smartly. There was a hard knot of pain on his right rib cage, where a burl of scar tissue reminded him of a newly healed wound. *Old man*, he thought. *You didn't take very good care of our body.*

Pepys looked up at him, an appraising expression on his tilted face. "At ease, Commander," he said.

It took a moment for former Lieutenant Storm to realize he'd achieved promotion in his lost years. He relaxed. The knot of pain slowly unraveled itself and went away after one or two jolts as he breathed. He'd been told he'd tackled a man in full dress battle armor with nothing but his hands. *There are old soldiers, and bold soldiers, but no old, bold soldiers*, he thought as Pepys stood up and trailed away, evidently expecting Jack to follow.

The privacy cubicle was barely large enough to hold a table and two chairs. There were white cup circle rings on the empty top. Pepys dropped into the larger chair, curling into it with the wiry grace of a small man. Jack took a look around before taking the second chair.

The emperor gave a little smile. "Old habits die hard."

"Habits?"

He waved a hand at the room. "No security in here. White sound screens up . . . no recording but our own fallible memories."

Jack felt uncomfortable. He *had* been searching for equipment, a reflex as unthought of as a sneeze or a yawn. Who had taught him to do such a thing?

Pepys patted the tabletop. "I'm told you've absolutely no memory of the last seven or eight years."

"I'm told the same thing," Jack answered wryly.

"Too bad. In the past you've worked both for me and—perhaps saying against me is too strong—for yourself. You must have thought it was worth it if you took the risk. As for myself, I'm pleased to be able to welcome you back into a time when the Knights have bccn not only resurrected but redeemed. There was a twenty year period when there was shame instead of glory. . . ."

Jack said nothing though the sudden tension in Pepys' languid form told him the emperor expected a reply. He had no memory with which to judge. "I'm told I have you to thank for that."

Pepys' intense gaze flickered a little. "Told, but not necessarily accepted. What can I say to put you at ease, my boy?"

Jack's muscles bunched. He knew instinctively he was not Pepys' boy. Though, if current memory served, he had sworn allegiance to Regis and this was Regis' successor. The audience chamber they sat in suddenly felt crowded, filled with dark and fleeting shadows. Pepys did not seem to notice them and, as Jack moved involuntarily away from them, they dissipated. *Ghosts,* he thought. *But whose?* "Tell me why we were in disgrace." And, as he watched a range of emotions move over the emperor's freckled visage, he knew why the Knights believed in a "Pure" war. The environment, the planet, must never suffer for the sins of the flesh that occupied it. Nine months and another Pepys could spring up to take the place of this one. But there would never be another Milos, or Dorman's Stand.

"Because you did not keep Milos," Pepys replied smoothly. "And as for the why—we hope you can tell us. Baadluster, in his capacity as Minister of War, will be here shortly, and then we'll move to a room where you can be recorded. You see, you're one of the few living survivors of that battle. The Thraks moved in so quickly, we have few tapes and documents of what actually happened." He held up a thin hand. "But you need only tell it once."

Jack could feel the thin sheen of sweat that had erupted suddenly across his forehead. They were asking for his nightmare and they *would* have it. So be it. What would they give him in exchange? His last few years? He doubted that. *Trust no one,* the disk had whispered in his ear. *If you would know the truth, find St. Colin.* "Then tell me about the Walker you want me to find."

"Ah." Pepys shifted in his chair, moving his weight from one hip to the other and leaning on the opposite arm. "We knew each other well once, before he became a Walker and went on his missionary way, and then became a saint. He's a good man and, damn it all, that's the basis of all this trouble. If he were not, we and the Walkers jockeying for position to replace him could be rid of him." Pepys grimaced at Jack's expression. "Speaking too frankly for you?"

Jack felt at a loss. He sensed the layers in the emperor's speech and knew that this man had reasons upon reasons for everything he did. As for Jack, he was just a foot soldier. Nothing more, and nothing less. His gut reacted for him. "A good man is worth the trouble."

Pepys sat upright in his chair. His hair fairly sparked as he ran a hand through it. Then he grinned as though the joke was upon himself. "Yes, I guess he is."

"The question would be," Jack added slowly, "why he hasn't come back on his own."

"What are you up against? Commander Storm, I think it likely you're up against nothing less than the Ash-farel. As recent as your emotions for the Thraks are, and despite the fact we've maintained a delicate balance of truce for years, the Ash-farel are the enemy now. We know nothing of them except that they come, they destroy, and they leave. We can't communicate with them and we haven't had much success fighting them, either. Whatever they are, they're fierce enough to have driven the Thraks into a swarming frenzy right down our throats."

Jack found the Ash-farel in his memory. The update tape, he supposed, for it was accompanied by emotionless pictorial records and nothing he'd personally experienced. Those records showed him planets cleaned of all life ... and yet, as he mulled the information over, he knew he saw a race which fought as he had been trained to fight. The planets themselves had not been damaged environmentally beyond a point where two or three years would see the worlds healed. Brutally efficient, like cleaning house without damaging the house itself. He'd seen what they'd done to shielded worlds. It was unlikely one crusader could have stood up to them, had he met them.

He crossed his legs and tapped the arch of his right shoe sole idly. "What is the likelihood," he asked, "of my finding Colin alive?"

"We both know it has to be none. Nor are you likely to even find relics enough to bring back— but Colin has never been a man to whom the expected happens. I think, I *feel*, he's still alive." Pepys leaned forward. "If you're to find him, you have to believe that, too."

"He has my armor."

"We believe so."

Jack tapped his foot harder. His armor had been contaminated, possibly still was. The berserker parasite inside was as big a menace to the holy man as the enemy he'd never met. "I'll need new armor."

"You've been fitted already. It's ready when you are."

"And volunteers." Jack gave a slight smile. "You brought me back as a traitor, a deserter. They may be a little difficult to find."

Pepys thrust himself abruptly out of his chair. "You told me you had no memory."

Jack stood, as well. Muscles, bones, and nerves

newly healed cried with dull pain, and he felt their weakness holding him back, but he still towered over the red-haired emperor. "I have none. But I have ears, and the guard you had on my doors talked. I don't know how I became a commander in your Knights, Pepys, or why I then decided to desert my duty, but I'm not so fresh out of the dirt fields that I will accept gullibly everything you tell me."

Pepys' mouth twitched. Then, amusement replaced the anger in his brilliant eyes. "Good men," he repeated wryly, "are a lot of trouble."

Vandover's appearance interrupted the emperor's quiet laugh at himself. The minister stood respectfully outside the chamber, but his shadow cast itself over them. Pepys stopped smiling. He leaned close and put a hand on Jack's forearm.

"I suggest," he said quietly, "that you trust to your memory and not to gossip when you speak in front of Baadluster." Then the emperor moved past him swiftly, saying, "Vandover! You're late."

"I had business, your highness, which detained me."

Jack watched the two of them bend their heads over the leaflet of plastisheets in Baadluster's hand and realized he could not hear what they softly discussed. And neither had Baadluster heard the emperor's last words to him. But his memory was flawed.

He was not a subtle man, but he felt the emperor had just told him that such a flaw might mean his life.

Chapter 9

The thrumming vibration brought him back to awareness. Bogie let his damped down sensors come back to full strength and his chamois self pumped in excitement as he recognized the approach of a major vessel. The coracle shuddered as it was captured once again. Bogie triggered open the shield door to the equipment bay. He stretched out his massive armored body and stood eagerly, waiting to hear Jack's voice broadcast.

But the com lines stayed quiet, except for a static chittering that he could not comprehend. The coracle quivered as if buffeted by a wind or tide and he could hear that it had been taken in, was now docked in a hold of some kind. Outside, vacuum was being bled away and air pumped in. He could feel the difference in the soundings through the hull.

He faced the main air lock, anticipating its opening.

His mission as a signpost to Colin's whereabouts was nearly fulfilled, but even more important, the expectation of a reunion with Jack warmed him. War had torn them away from each other, but Bogie had never doubted that fate would bring them together again. Helmet visor forward, he scanned the portal eagerly.

But it was not opened, it was blown away. The armor rocked back on its heels, sensors flooded by heat and the blast—and the nightmare Kabuki-mask faces of the invaders as they climbed in, their chitin aglow in the explosion's wake.

He'd been found all right, but by Thraks.

If memory served him, Jack would have showed his teeth grimly and waded in, suit gauntlets laying down a line of fire.

Bogie brought his arms up. He'd circumvented his safety and had been fully weaponed for some time. Now he activated the Dead Man circuit so that if they pulled him down, the suit would not last beyond the first crack in its sealing. These were the enemy.

He aimed and strode forward.

Chapter 10

It was like putting on a shabby, beloved old coat with pockets full of memories and past humiliations, all indivisible from one another. Or maybe it was like sitting on an alien beach, letting brilliantly colored sand run through her fingers and trying to decide if one color was good and another bad—there was no real way to separate them or make a judgment. And what if the most beautifully colored grain was perhaps the end result of the most terrible memory? Would she, now that all was said and done, throw it away?

Amber lay in quietude, her chest barely moving under its sheeted cover, feeling her life in all its layers, her mind far more active than her body yet still aware of her awakening state. Memory came back like feeling . . . prickly, painful, yet welcome pins and needles. She felt her breath bolt through her lungs and issue out in discharge, chilled by her still, cold interior. She began to shake, teeth chattering.

A nurse appeared, warmed blanket in her arms, and tucked it around Amber. She checked her ankle shunt to make sure Amber had not kicked off the dialysis shunt, murmured an encouraging sound and passed on. Amber barely noticed her. Her mind was too busy.

Like a kaleidoscope, the shards of her life fell and tumbled about her, pretty pictures with sharp edges, and yesterday was among them. She had lost nothing and gained everything. As the warmth of the blanket penetrated, she closed her eyes and slept a second time.

"He's yours," Vandover said quietly. He squeezed his hands together slightly, the only movement which betrayed his emotions. "He has no memory of your previous agreement and so, therefore—"

"Neither should I," finished Pepys. "Think you?"

"Think? He scarcely blinked in debriefing. He holds you in the proper respect and awe a recruit might be expected to . . . we should have thought of this long ago. Storm defused, but still valuable to us."

"Yes." Pepys tapped a curved fingernail against the teeth of his smile. "And now he's going after Colin because *I* command him to, and not because of their friendship. I'm in control now."

"Which is as it should be." Vandover paced beyond the seated emperor, turned and came back. "It worked as I told you it would."

"I am glad," his emperor returned. He looked up with his verdant eyes. "If not, you would have killed him, wouldn't you?"

"No. But I would have had him killed, for you." Vandover took a deep breath. "He's still dangerous. He doesn't like being manipulated."

Pepys waved a negligent hand. "An emperor commands."

Vandover nodded. He paused in the doorway as Pepys added, "What about the girl?"

"She's mine."

Pepys inclined his head, indicating his answer. "As we discussed."

"Then I will do nothing, for the moment. Although he doesn't know her, he has an almost . . . instinctual recollection of her. I've seen it in his eyes. Why create suspicion unnecessarily if she disappears too suddenly?"

"And if she corrupts him?"

Vandover's lips tightened. "She'll never get that close to him again. Now, your highness . . . I have other appointments."

"Of course. Don't let me keep you any longer."

Baadluster gave an abbreviated bow and left the chamber. Though he quickly turned down a right-angle corridor and left the chamber far behind, he could still feel the emperor's burning gaze upon his back.

His own chambers were much more somber than those of Pepys' and dominated by readouts and listings of the skirmishes between humans, Thraks, and Ash-farel. The Triad Throne took pride in its mercenary troops, but the news was not favorable. The clandestine activity between Thraks and humans was showing an ominous up-trend. Nor was he any closer to pinpointing the origins of the Ash-farel or to predicting their patterns of aggression.

Vandover frowned, looking closely at his

screening of the latest graphics. Did Pepys not fully comprehend the danger? If so, why did the emperor continue his dance with the Walkers? What could a threatening civil war possibly avail him at this point?

He scanned the information he had posted, knowing that there was a pattern here, if he could but decipher it. He opened his com line to the aide-de-camp on watch.

"Sir?"

"Make an appointment with Commander K'rok for tomorrow."

"Yes, sir."

Vandover sat back in his chair. The Milot kept his thoughts close to his chest, but there was information to be had there if one was skillful enough. Bridging the gap between the emperor's mercenary troops and those of the Thraks, as K'rok was technically a Thrak himself, left the Milot in a position to discern happenings even the Minister of War was unlikely to know. Unraveling K'rok would be a challenge. He bridged his fingers over his nose and sank deeper into thought.

He swung about in his chair to find out he was not alone.

"Good evening, Baadluster."

She had dressed in black and a blue so deep in color its iridescent shimmer was almost black. He didn't see her at first, not until she moved out of the shadows of the corners. Even then he would not have seen her except that she was in motion. Her tawny mane had been tamed: combed and braided at the nape of her neck. She moved with a confidence that inflamed his blood and raised the bile in his gorge at the same time. Vandover halted, gathering his thoughts.

"I was going to send a car for you."

She perched on the corner of the desk console. "I was ready to leave tonight. I saw no reason not to." She turned the full attention of her amber gaze on him.

Vandover felt a quickening in his guts. The fire to his spark was there now, he saw it in her. How could he not have seen it before, the psychic energy that coursed through her body as hotly as her blood? Yes, she had dimmed it, banked it, possibly had even quenched it; now he had brought it back to life. It was as though he had created her anew.

Amber leaned close. She wore a subtle perfume that was perhaps no more than the shampoo scent in her hair. He responded in spite of himself. "I wanted you to know," she said softly, "that it would be dangerous for you to think we have a partnership or that I will be grateful for what you've done for me."

His ardor chilled, but not his pleasure. Vandover allowed himself to smile. "Milady," he answered, "you underestimate us both."

She stood abruptly. Tensile strength replaced slender grace. "I'm done playing games with you. You call me 'milady,' but your voice says 'whore.' I'm not yours to jack around, Vandover, and I've come to remind you of that fact. I'm going back to Jack and whether he remembers me or not is immaterial. I'll fight for what's mine."

He got to his feet. "Commendable. Commendable and predictable. But do you think this is safe, declaring yourself and drawing a battle line be-

tween the two of us? Are you really so sure that
we are done with alliance?"

"I'm sure."

It was late in the palace. The nighttime lighting
from the corridors glowed into the room. Vandover reached out to his console and keyed the
chamber doors shut and locked. Amber took a step
back, but high color outlined her cheekbones as
the chamber lights came up.

"Now," he said, "we may speak privately."

"If you think those doors will hold me—"

Vandover laughed. "You'll stay, and not because of the doors or even locks."

Her gaze narrowed. "I could kill you," she told
him.

He laughed again, genuine mirth filling him. "I
know!" he said triumphantly. "How well I know!
I'm the one who had you programmed!"

Chapter 11

Amber recoiled from him. The control and menace that had been hers now suddenly became
Baadluster's. She took a breath. He couldn't know.
She fought for composure and found it. Before,
she had been close to killing the minister for
Jack's sake. Now it meant her own survival. "What
do you mean?"

"I mean that you should not threaten me. I know
who and what you are. I know your innermost secret. I have the key." Vandover swung away from
her and paced the chamber's length, checking the
door seal before turning back to her. "We have
things to say in private."

"I have nothing to say to you!"

"No? Then perhaps you'll listen. Even Rolf did
not know which was the genuine trigger I had in-
stilled in your neuro-lingal programming. My
wishes are buried so deeply, so subliminally,
you'll never know what makes you kill. Do you
want to hear it, Amber? Are you ready to fulfill
your destiny?" He still smiled widely. Then, as if
reading her thoughts, added, "And what do you
want to bet I can trigger you before you can kill
me?"

She unclenched her fists. With studied movements, she returned to the console where she had been perched before and resettled herself. She caught the momentary hesitation in his eyes. He couldn't be sure . . . just as she couldn't. "Why do you think I contain this . . . trigger?"

"You belonged to the pack of street kids Rolf had working for him."

"Half of under-Malthen could probably make that claim."

The light in Vandover's eyes seemed to flare. "This is no claim. Jack defended you from him on several occasions until the man was killed."

She shrugged.

"I hired Rolf to find me an assassin. Not just a street lethal child to be groomed—I wanted a special child. I wanted one with abilities difficult to measure."

Amber tilted her head, listening. She found herself unwilling to meet the blaze in his eyes any longer. She did not want him to see the despair she felt was undeniably in her own.

"Shall I describe those abilities to you?" Vandover licked his lips. "Cunning, of a surety, but then almost any feral child on Malthen's streets has cunning. Quickness and glibness, too. And a temper to match the tongue. Do you recognize yourself yet, my lovely Amber? Do you?"

She felt the hatred warm in her, running like a hot wire just under her skin. Her hair felt heavy upon the back of her neck. As she reached up and began to loosen it from its bonds, the knife in her wrist sheath flexed uncomfortably to remind her of its presence.

"Shall I continue?"

Amber paused, her hands up, fingers unknotting

her hair. "No," she said softly. "I'm not the one you think I am."

"I know you are. Rolf had his tastes and desires, he did. He preferred children. He told me once just how he'd found his candidate for my assassin." Baadluster came close, closer, weight balanced on the balls of his feet. "He'd tried to rape the child, and found himself knocked on his ass for it. Psychically, not physically. The child had made himself unapproachable. That's what threw me for a number of years when I began to search for the information myself. A simple matter of gender."

Her glance flickered up in spite of herself, in spite of the man's heat which crested higher and higher. His voice pounded at her. "But I kept searching. You should thank me for my diligence, really. If it were not for your new-found usefulness to me. . . ."

Her hair freed, she dropped her hands to her lap, slender fingers close to the cuff of the sleeve which hid her knife. "You have no proof."

"Shall we see if you can be raped?"

"I'll kill you first." The calm breaths she had been forcing now grew ragged.

"Perhaps." He leaned closer. "But not before I can speak the words you fear most. You will do that which horrifies you most. You will murder without cause or need."

The knife handle was so close to her fingertips she could sense its field. "I would never kill for you."

"You'd have no choice!" Vandover spun away. "Get out of here. Go to the man who commands your heart. I've got the rest of you now, body and soul." He touched the console and the doors opened.

She paused at the door. "You're wrong."

"No," he said softly, menacingly. "I saw it within you. You're mine, milady, and I will have satisfaction."

Amber fled into the abandoned corridor.

He dreamed of a dark-eyed angel. Not the softly rounded, beneficent angel he'd seen depicted in the paintings in the Walker compound. No, this one raged with righteous justice, her white robes torn and ragged as storm winds held her aloft on spread wings which were as shot with dark and lightning as the tempest. Her hair spread about her angry face almost like a second pair of wings and the glory of the anger in those dark eyes—

Jack jerked awake, thinking of Amber. In the lightless confines of his apartment, he thought he saw her, dressed in her favorite blue caftan of By-thian make, her fair skin tattooed with the vein-like, intricate patterns the shaman and prophet had drawn upon her. She drifted toward him, arms opening for an embrace and he, desire quickening, sat up to take her in.

As quickly as the memory touched him, it fled. He sat on his soldier's bunk, the mattress hard under his lean buttocks, grasping at thin air, unaware of what he was doing.

Then, dizzily, the memories came back. He was not one man but two, yet they were the same. His mouth cottoned. He put one foot on the floor to steady himself. His pulse thundered through his skull and then quieted. He *knew*, and knowing that, understood that his life and those of the people he loved were in even more danger.

Pepys had warned him. Had Pepys known that his memories would overlay themselves and begin to integrate again?

They had tampered with him, Pepys and Vandover. Had one conspired to undo the machinations of the other? Rage filled him. He tore the bedsheets aside and swung his other leg out of bed, body in motion before his mind had even decided on vengeance. The touch of his warm foot on the cold floor stilled him. The bastards couldn't leave him alone. He was not even left time to savor the long-lost memories of his home and family, now restored.

A ghost stirred in the corner of his apartment, saying gently, "You still don't sleep at night." Amber came toward him, inseparable from the shadows that hid her, except for the soft illumination that highlighted her face and golden-brown hair. There was as much hate as love in her expression.

"How did you get in here?"

Sadness curtained the other's emotion. "You used to remember how I do things like this."

He wanted to tell her that he *knew*, and couldn't. It knotted in his chest. Until he understood what had happened to him during imprint, and what schemes his emperor had entangled him in, he would only endanger her as well. He made his face go blank and could only hope that his eyes did not mirror his thoughts. "Should I remember that you're a thief?"

She sat down at the foot of the bed, crossed her legs limberly, and propped her chin in the palm of one hand. "You sound like you've been talking to Vandover." She wore black with a dark blue shimmering, and he thought of ravens' wings, flashing as the birds flew over his father's fields on Dorman's Stand.

"I've been talking to a lot of people these past few days. You're the only one who seems to be an expert on my sleeping habits, however." The desire which had faded since his first awakening gave him a dull throb.

Her gaze searched his face. "You really don't know me, do you?"

"No."

For the briefest moment, it took both of her hands to hold her face. Then she seemed to gather herself and looked up again.

Suddenly, Jack knew what Colin described as hell. He could not comfort her. He could not brush away whatever demons she was struggling with, and he knew that she was fighting a mighty battle somewhere within herself. He knew it because his love for her told him and yet he dared not help her fight that battle.

The moment passed and Amber took a deep breath. "We're a fine pair," she said, with a touch of bitterness, "to think about saving worlds."

"I'm just a foot soldier," he said, to his own surprise, and knew his younger, restored self, was speaking. "I do what I can."

Amber thrust herself to her feet. "I'd better go now, before I find myself suggesting that I try unorthodox methods to remind you who I am."

"I wouldn't mind," Jack said, and felt himself smiling in the darkness of the bedroom.

"I'm sure you wouldn't." Amber leaned forward and kissed him. Her lips were hard and fervent.

Then she stepped back. "Somewhere inside of you, buried, it has to be buried because I can't accept the fact that it's gone, somewhere inside of you is the man I love who loves me."

Jack cleared his throat. "If he comes back, you'll be the first to know."

She eyed him fiercely a second longer. "I hope so. Because we both need him desperately." She turned, and then she was gone, almost as if she had never been there.

Jack fisted his hand. "Damn!" His voice sounded gravelly, choked by the knotted emotions he'd kept back. Amber was in trouble and he was unable to help her. He spoke to the night. "Your throne's not enough anymore, Pepys. I want your guts for this one."

Chapter 12

There is life in prayer, Colin thought, the hard mat of the flooring pounding new bruises upon the bruises already on his knees. He reflected also that the pain of it might add more potency though he normally found prayer very comforting. Now it was the only conversation he had, and as he levered himself off the cell floor and laborously sat down upon a crude three-legged stool he had manufactured, he wondered idly if his captors had been recording him.

He spoke aloud constantly to facilitate their knowledge of his language, but he'd never been given any sign that they were even hearing beings. He could not reach them or if he did reach them, they cared little. Why then did they keep him? What did they see when they looked at him?

Colin sat within his cell, watching his dim, obfuscated reflection stare back. The walls, ceiling, and floor were of a material he was not familiar with: light as plastic sheets, but metallic and enduringly tough. Because of the material, he thought he was in a temporary holding area that, like a tent, might be folded and taken down when not needed. He wondered how long he might be allowed to prolong that need.

He spread his hands over his aching knees and rubbed gingerly. The bones and sinews showed clearly. He was losing flesh. The Ash-farel recognized in him a need to eat and drink and flush his system accordingly, but never gave him enough. His mouth was constantly dry and his lips chapped. He felt hunger almost as intensely as the pain of his wounds.

"You are," he told himself, "a foolish old man." The warmth of his spare hands lent him some comfort, but it would not last.

It was vanity that had sent him to the Ash-farel, a sin of the ego for which he was now being punished. He could expect no less. He had thought to communicate when no one else had, yet what conceit had told him he could? He had thought to quell a war, yet left behind him a situation poised on the precipice of civil insurrection.

"Always clean your own house first," he murmured, still watching as he kneaded the aches and pains of his joints. Jonathan would be furious with him for both the state of his health and his garments. He wore scarcely more than rags though the cell seemed to be kept at a temperature that warranted little clothing anyway.

Colin had tried every method he could conceive of to communicate with: sight, sound, color, scent, even music. The only reaction he had ever garnered was when he had been initially taken and they had begun to dispose of him as though he was a particularly squishy and pestiferous bug. He had fought back with every fiber until they had finally contained him and then jailed him. The efforts he'd gone through to get a chamber pot and then food had practically killed him.

Small triumphs, Colin thought, as he rubbed his knees a last time. It was God's will that he could be triumphant at all. Pepys was right. He had forgotten his humble beginnings, where it was a victory just to grow up fed and clothed and sheltered. It sobered him. Perhaps he had been seeking for the Kingdom of God in all the wrong places.

He smiled to himself. A lesson learned late was better than no lesson learned at all.

Chapter 13

"We've located Denaro," Vandover said, self-satisfaction evident in his tone.

"Where?"

The man in black bowed in deference to his emperor. "In the Outward Bounds. He's leaving a clear trail."

"As predicted. He wants to draw Storm after him." Pepys scratched the side of his head, and his aureole of red hair crackled with energy as he did so. "The only surprise here is that it's taken you so long to find him. Is it confirmed?"

"Yes."

"Then be sure Jack gets the word as well."

"He'll be even more ready to leave than he is now."

Pepys gave a brief, bittersweet smile. "Be assured, Vandover, that I intend to send him on his way as soon as I can. I want the audience hall opened up again. Let every legitimate spokesperson for the Walkers in."

Baadluster's jaw fell agape. Then, "But your highness—"

"If I don't let them in, they'll beat the doors down sooner or later. I rule here, not the mob. This is a throne room, not a boardroom. Let's see if we can't put Storm in the forefront and let him take some of the heat."

"The Walkers want your blood," Vandover responded. "I don't advise this, if for no other reason than we want to keep the commander inaccessible."

"He's my shield man, and as such, I can't afford to keep him inaccessible."

"What about the Green Shirts?"

Pepys shrugged. "They've chosen to blend in with the Walker factions—if we can placate the Walkers, the Shirts cannot afford to step out of line. Not now. We're too close to declaring martial law and that could hamper their operations here severely. No, they'll be somewhat circumspect." He met Baadluster's gaze. "Don't you think?"

Vandover thought that the emperor had webs of his own that he knew nothing of, and he did not like it. He considered the idea that Pepys had come to the end of his own usefulness. The palms of his hands itched as he hid his thoughts. "Put that way, I agree."

"Good. Make whatever arrangements with the WP and the sweepers that you have to. I don't want the barracks or training grounds breached."

"I'll make the arrangements," Vandover told him. Without seeming to be hasty, he brought the conversation to a close and bowed his way out. Nothing in the emperor's cold stare told him that the tone of his voice had been far from subservient.

"I'd give my left nut to g' with you, boy, but that's not my lot." The chunky sergeant strolled alongside Jack, his beefy legs stretching to keep up with Storm's stride.

Jack smiled. "And take you away from the recruits? Pepys would have *my* left nut if I suggested it." In rapid time, they reached the cornerstone of the base, and stopped where the massive walls closed off the parade and training grounds, and where the shop buildings abutted the structure. He *knew* the grounds and yet did not . . . his memories slip-sliding over one another as though he looked through a camera obscura. One moment he knew exactly who he was and where he'd been; the next moment his mind was as blank as an unwritten page.

Lassaday cleared his throat. "I'm glad we got all that traitor and deserter stuff put behind us."

Jack turned from the parade walls and looked down at the NCO. "That's politics, Sarge. Pepys and Vandover and who knows who else—and I don't guarantee that it's behind us at all."

The white-hot Malthen sun glinted off Lassaday's well-bronzed pate. He showed his teeth. "Them things can trip up an honest soldier good, Commander." He jerked a thumb to the walls. "Rawlins'll be dismissed in another couple of minutes. I've got to get the racks out for the suits."

"I'll be fine," Jack reassured him. The NCO hesitated, then awkwardly rolled back into motion, leaving him alone and on his honor, as it were. Pepys did not exactly have Jack under house arrest, but neither had his status been cleared up. Storm would find himself exonerated if and when he found Colin.

It was as though he had blinked, looking after

the NCO, and he found himself grasping after thoughts he no longer had under control. Jack shuddered and his palms grew sweaty as he fought the panic of being in an unknown area for unknown reasons. His body had brought him here and then abandoned him, and he knew . . . he knew that he was losing his mind. He steadied himself and, like a fading echo, remembered that he was here to meet someone.

He looked at the towering walls. He could hear a rumbling of distant warfare beyond them and then dulled silence. Maneuvers. He recognized the muffled sound of battle armor in use and smiled, remembering. Armor he *knew*. Armor was more than a second skin to him. He anticipated the tunnel opening and the men spilling out, the suits encasing them with a kind of power and grace foot soldiers had never thought to have. Mobile tanks, redesigned, sleeked down and yet massive. *No suit, no soldier*, he thought, as if his own days of training had been yesterday.

He shuddered a last time, just before the portals opened.

The soldier who approached him wore captain's insignia on his chest plate, and had his helmet off, hooked on his equipment belt. The battle armor smelled of fire and dirt and sweat. As Jack's eyes met those of the captain, he knew with a jolt that this man was an undiluted version of himself: piercing dark blue eyes, wheat-blond hair, steadily looking back at him. Sweat streaked his temples and dripped down the back of his neck. The young captain had been hard at work. He put a gauntlet out.

"Commander, it's good to see you again."

Jack took the gauntlet without hesitation, though he knew the power behind the suit could easily crush his hand. He also knew that a soldier wearing armor knew what he was doing. "Captain."

Behind them, recruits were thundering to the shop and the equipment racks Lassaday had set up. They were sweaty also, and tired to the bone, but the suits came first. The suits always came first. Once his armor was cleaned and serviced, a trooper could go home and soak his own weary muscles.

One yelled out as he went past, "Rawlins!" to which the young captain responded, "Later, Corporal," and turned his attention back to Jack.

Rawlins. Jack knew he should probably know this man intimately. He'd been an aide to Storm once. He grasped for recall and found nothing. Then it was there, briefly, like a wisp of cloud across the face of a too-hot sun: a faded scene of another world, Rawlins with blood on him, but whole, supporting a man he knew as St. Colin, as they walked through a carnage of Thrakian and otherworldly dead. What was the connection between the two of them? He found nothing else, but this memory at least stayed with him. He tucked it away. *I'll have you yet, all of you.*

Rawlins drew him aside. "Thanks for meeting with me, Commander. I wanted to talk to you first, before I did anything official."

"All right. I'm listening."

The young man unhooked his helmet from his belt and studied it, speaking quietly. "I want to go with you. I want to volunteer to find St. Colin."

Why the secrecy? Was Rawlins afraid Jack would refuse? Should Jack fear the tenuous connection between them? He studied the captain. He had nothing to go on but his gut feelings, and his instincts told him that this was an honorable man.

"If it can be arranged, Captain, I'd be pleased," he found himself saying.

Pleasure and determination flashed from those piercing eyes as Rawlins glanced up. "That's all I can ask, sir," the man answered.

"Is it?"

Rawlins' gaze dropped back to the helmet again and he seemed to be examining it minutely. "You could have your doubts about me, sir. I've been known to obey Colin instead of you, sir."

"Pepys could say the same about me. There are times when a good soldier has no choice but to disobey." He felt a tingling of knowledge within himself. There were times when a good soldier had no choice but mutiny. The truth of it rang throughout his very fiber like a clarion call. This was who he was—

Rawlins' voice interrupted his thought. "Commander K'rok," he finished.

Jack blinked. "Of course," he said. "I'll speak to him."

Rawlins relaxed and saluted. "Thank you, sir. I'll be waiting for you to make arrangements."

Storm saluted back and watched the young man leave, leonine grace in Flexalinks, his bared head a flaxen beacon. He thought of K'rok, the Milot commander of the Knights. He had no desire to meet with a smelly, hirsute, devious Milot. Another frame slid over his thoughts—hand to hand with the Milot, face to snarling face—and respect as well as defeat in the eyes of the other.

Jack clenched his hand, feeling a minor ache where his finger had been sheared off. Reaching for those elusive memories did no good; the harder he tried to grasp them, the more slippery they got. He thought of St. Colin and of resurrection. Beyond his orders from Pepys, there grew in him the burning need to find the man for himself. There would be truth and resurrection when he did. He stood staring after the battle suits as they carried their wearers thundering across the expanse and thought of his own suit, infected, dangerous to any who might covet it. There was a canker that needed to be cauterized as soon as possible. He was to claim his new armor later that day. He would have to remember to put out the word that the old suit was to be destroyed as soon as it was located.

Jack pivoted and returned to the dusky rose confines of the obsidite-walled palace.

When the summons came that was not a request but an order, Amber was ready. She chafed at the call, but did not flinch away because she had been prepared for it. Baadluster had her on a leash, it was axiomatic that he would yank it whenever he felt like reminding her. But the despair had given way to action, and she dressed for the meeting with a calm determination, secreting the circuitry and explosives about her body with special attention so that scanners and her dress would not give her away. There was a serenity to each of her movements, each placement of a tiny packet that would not raise alarm of itself, but combined with

every other packet would be enough to vaporize
Baadluster and anyone else within five feet of her
when she triggered the detonator. Vandover might
know that she was wired. Dealing with it would
be another matter altogether. Nothing he could do
could stop her.

It was strange that the decision had given her
such calm. She smoothed the drape of her red
dress over her hip. The fabric was lush and silken,
its color the deep full ruby of blood. She looked
at her face in the mirror—her hair thick and curling about her slender face with the chin she'd always thought too pointed—and retraced a pout
about her lips. The open sensuality of the expression she made would hit Vandover like a fist below the belt. She intended it to. By the time the
man recovered, it would be too late.

She patted the powder along her eyelids into
a sultry shadow and straightened. The spidery
webbing of the gossamer wires along her bare
skin could not be detected under her dress's fine
lines. She'd had some trouble smuggling in the
goods. Malthen was a city under siege. The
striking Walkers had closed down most busi-
nesses and even the Green Shirts had been
damned hard to reach. But she still had her con-
nections in under-Malthen and they'd served her
well.

Amber blew a kiss at her reflection before turning away. The only ripple in her calm happened
when she thought of Jack—Jack, whom she could
no longer help and who could not help her. She
swallowed down the lump in her throat. He would
never forgive her for this. That would be her own
private hell.

She felt a dampness at the corner of her eye and quickly put a fingertip to it, blotting it out. "I will *not* cry. Not any more." She keyed open her door and left before her determination failed her.

Chapter 14

Colin pushed away his gourd bowl in disgust. The steamed vegetable, which usually was his container and dinner in one, held what appeared to be a mass of squirming maggots. Hungry though he was, the wriggling knot of flesh turned his stomach. For reasons he could only attribute to the eating habits of his captors, these meals arrived sporadically. Usually he could not identify the living parasites that inhabited the gourd—the varieties changed from time to time—though crickets and maggots were close enough the last two times. Yet even though his stomach had shrunken terribly, he could not bring himself to eat what he had been given. Cooked perhaps—no, never. His resolve wavered as he shoved the gourd back through the door flap from which it had appeared.

He sat on his haunches and hugged his knees and tried not to think of the time span which might elapse before his next meal arrived. Once or twice, they had speedily given him new food, but most often they did not. He wondered if he insulted them by refusing his dinner even as his stomach growled in bitter protest. Food seemed to be the only common ground they had.

He felt a rumbling underneath him. For a moment, he thought that the clenching and growling of his hunger shook his entire body, then he knew that his cell responded to something else.

The walls shook. Colin got clumsily to his feet. He grabbed up his stool for whatever protection it might afford him as his cell peeled apart and he stood blinking in the harsh floodlights.

The Ash-farel had come seeking him.

He had seen the Ash-farel mummified on the dead moon of Lasertown. He'd walked among their remains on Colinada and detected their presence in Walker prehistory sites. He had not known then who or what he dealt with, but even a thousand thousand years dead, they had been magnificent.

Now he quailed before the three who faced him, his thoughts and rational reasoning blown from his mind by winds of awe and terror. Angels, he thought for a moment, inspired such feelings. And devils. Then even those reflections were driven from him.

They were massive, three times his size, and undoubtedly saurian, but the scales of their skin were jewels that bedazzled his eyes, and their limbs were supple and quick, their eyes coals of fire that lanced his soul. They emanated righteous anger and he dropped to his knees, the crude stool he would have used for protection rolling out of numbed fingers. As they reached for him, his heart fluttered wildly in his chest.

"Oh, God," he cried out, knowing that he was dying, for if they did not kill him, surely his heart was bursting in his chest. He twisted his head to see where they carried him, and when he saw, prayed that he might be lucky enough to die first. The glittering sterility of table equipment, lights, and tools met his eyes.

As alien as these beings were, the man knew a vivisection lab when he saw one. He began to kick and scream helplessly.

Chapter 15

Vandover had his back to the chamber doors when they opened. "Milady," he said, without turning. Amber cast a quick glance about the spacious private rooms: anteroom and library, and doors to the bedroom beyond, apartments nearly as gracious as those of the emperor himself. The chambers occupied the penthouse floor. Behind Baadluster was an unobstructed skyline view of the palace grounds and Malthen. The windows were glass, offering a crystalline sharp view to the horizon. Amber preferred plastic, the slight fuzziness of which lent a softer aspect to the cityscape.

On the other hand, glass could be kicked through a lot quicker. Smiling slightly to herself, she advanced far enough into the room to allow the doors to glide shut behind her.

Vandover turned. As quickly as his eyes widened to take her in, his gaze narrowed. "Milady," he repeated. Then, "Have you forgotten I have no heart?"

"Seduction," Amber said, moving closer, "doesn't rely on heart. And you do lust, Minister, I see it in your eyes. For power and . . . other things."

His mouth closed with a nearly audible snap. He had been working hard that day. Purple bruises of fatigue shadowed his dark eyes and his pasty complexion looked paler than usual. Whatever she expected him to say, it wasn't what he said next.

"I am the master here."

Amber felt her cheeks grow hot, knew that color tinged her face. She inclined her head in silence and waited, fearing that she had made him suspicious. Only let him come close enough for her to be sure that she would take him with her!

But he did not approach her. He kept his distance across the room and she felt his scrutiny, felt his rough probe that she fended off, being careful not to give away her power in relation to his—and wondered if he played the same game. Surely he could not be very powerful or else she would have sensed him years ago . . . and feared him.

It had been a long time since she had known fear. Oh, she had worried about Jack and herself many a time, but the strength-leeching fear that trying to survive on the streets brought, she hadn't felt that since leaving Rolf. She knew it now.

"I do not always have to be the master, but I will not play the game," he said, his voice as hollow as if it issued from a tomb. "I will not promise you that you can be my partner. We both know that is not your price."

Her mouth went dry as she whispered, "Jack is my price," and found to her shock that Vandover said it at the same time.

"Jack is your price." He paused. "I can't promise you his safety either. There are too many others involved in the struggle for this empire. But if he stays without his current memories, I can promise you that I won't be the one who calls for his death."

She looked up. There was both hope and damnation in his words. And the threat that she could be the one he called upon to end Jack's life if he came to that decision. "No," she said. "That's not good enough."

He shrugged. His robes rustled upon his lanky frame with the movement. "It's all I can offer. I can compel you whether you wish it or not."

"Not to kill Jack!"

He had a drink in one hand. He raised it now to sip at. "My dear girl," he said, but his voice took an ugly tone and Amber knew he may have voiced girl, but he thought *whore*. "You'll do whatever I trigger you to."

"Over my dead body." She threw herself at him, one hand to claw at him and the other grasping at the detonator hidden in the necklace she wore.

He caught her. Glass crashed to the apartment floor and shattered, then ground to deadly shards beneath their shoes as he bent back her arms. He showed his teeth.

Amber brought her knee up. He gasped and let her go, then quickly recaptured her left wrist as she twisted and tried to grasp the pendant again. Breathing quickly, harshly, he said, "What do you have planned, milady, eh?"

He forced her back, tripping over the edge of her dress which gave way with a loud rip. The wall caught her up sharply. Amber flinched as the wiring ground into her skin.

Vandover pressed into her, grinding her into the

wall. She felt him quickening into hardness as their bodies clashed. His breath thickened. He pinioned her wrists above her head with one hand. She twisted and strove to free herself, but he was far stronger than she could ever have guessed. He stroked a wing of hair that had fallen loose upon her cheek.

"What trap have you set for me? Will you tell me?"

Despite the hardness that thrust at her, she leaned into him. Let their chests meet severely enough and the blow would set off the detonator.

He drew back a little warily, his face flushed. He caught her under the chin and held her face cupped in his hand, his hand which was as steely strong as the one bruising her wrists.

"Talk to me!"

Her teeth ground together. She parted her lips in contempt. "I will . . . never . . . murder for you!"

The heel of his hand stopped her words and she felt blood in her mouth, tasted its sudden leap. He thrust his pelvis into her and her stomach turned at the touch of his manhood, the silken fineness of her dress scant shield against him. The traitorous wall held her pressed to him.

"Remember," he said harshly. "You came to me."

Her mind erupted of its own accord, forgetting her suicide, the detonator, the explosives, the fine circuitry she wore like a web of undergarments. He would never have her. Psychic fire lashed out. She struck and struck deep, unheeding that he might yet have time to say the words she feared most. Her thoughts speared him. She poured her-

self into her attack until her very soul threatened
to leave her body.

Lights exploded. Articles began to rise in the air
and smash across the room. Pictures toppled from
their moorings. Furniture danced in its place,
stampeding upon the floor. Books took wing from
the massive bookcases. The air filled with sound
and fury and then the flying objects began to spi-
ral inward until an immense maelstrom of destruction filled the center of the chamber.

When she realized what she had done, she held
her breath, waiting.

Vandover staggered back a half step. The lust
burning in his eyes went blank. His cruel mouth
slackened. Their pelvises separated. His iron bar
of a leg kept her own pinned or she would have
kicked free.

Amber inhaled with a quavering sound. His
hand should weaken on her wrists. She twisted,
expecting the convulsion of death to break her free
altogether.

His mouth fell open. He gasped for air. Then
light flickered back into Vandover's eyes. The eddy
whirling overhead began to settle, drifting gently
to earth, tamed. The din quieted until all that
could be heard was the sound of the books fluttering and then slapping to the ground.

He rocked back on his heels and roared with
laughter. When he had done, he jerked her into
his rough embrace. "Like fire you are," he told
her. "But I am water. Deep and still. Muddied and
polluted, perhaps. My power has always been feeble, but it feeds on yours. Feed me, Amber. Feel
me grow stronger."

Fear lanced through her. Her breasts crushed

against his chest. "Let me go!" Amber spat. She jerked and kicked, desperate to reach the pendant that would destroy him and set her free.

Their struggle rent open the neckline of her gown. His calloused fingers grabbed for her breast and pinched her nipple. It tightened under his touch. Amber snapped at his face, but even as Vandover flinched away, he saw the spidery network of wires her gown had been concealing.

He tore the necklace from her throat. It took flesh with it. She let out a sound of pain as he threw her back against the wall and pinned her there, one massive hand clawlike upon her throat, so tight she could scarely breathe. Black spots swam before her eyes.

Amber caught the sob before it could sound.

The pendant cupped in the palm of his hand, he clawed at her dress and ripped it away savagely, shred by shred. Ruby threads and patches drifted to the floor like pieces of flesh. Her skin grew cold and her pulse roared in her ears. Choked into submission, she leaned against the wall, helpless as he bared her body. His fingers probed and pinched at her until her nipples stood out in purple anger and her body throbbed in violation.

He tore the last fragment of her silkspun panties from her. With it, the last adhesive patch of explosive from her skin. He tossed it and the necklace pendant aside. He let her drop to her knees.

He knelt beside her on one knee. His left hand squeezed her throat tighter yet, and he stroked the inside of her thighs with the back of his right hand. "You would have killed us both," he said. His voice thickened. Amber thrashed feebly, her vision blinded, her limbs grown weak. "You won't defy me again."

He let go of her and she sagged into his arms. With a low, guttural sound, he let her drop to the floor. As she cried for breath, he stripped himself. She felt the heat from him scald her own chilled body. Then the power of his mind took her up and bound her as tightly as if he had used chains. Every attack she sent against him, he absorbed and turned back against her until she could do nothing but lie helplessly still, a prisoner of her own mind.

He raped her then. But not quickly, so that it might be over and done. He lingered over her, using and knowing every part of her, so that nothing of her might be untouched by him. So that nothing of herself might remain hers. So that nothing that might ever be touched by anyone else would ever forget the memory of his touch, his pain, his faint pleasure.

So that she might hate herself forever.

His kisses branded her. He whispered dull obscenities as he worked on her. He brought her flesh to life so that she moaned in spite of herself, knowing the edge of desire which he turned to pain, and then he started over again. He licked the salt sweat and sweet blood from her skin as if it was honey. When he was done with her mouth, her lips were swollen and throbbing, but she could not force a cry from them.

And when finally he was sated, he lay beside her and took her in his arms and felt her body shudder uncontrollably in shock and then he put his moist lips to her ear and whispered the name of the first person she must murder. Then he loosened his bondage so that she might cry and struggle weakly against him.

When she had done with sobbing, he took her again. Then he told her that she would do whatever he wanted willingly, or the next name he spoke would be Jack's.

Chapter 16

Nightime. Sensors adjusted to delicate shadows could not find the silent figure moving with a strange, broken grace just outside their range. Alarms that were keyed to weaponry passed over the figure without sounding any warning. With caution, the stalker ranged throughout the complex, lighted and dark, until it found its destination and paused, to watch unseen.

A woman sat and eyed her face in her mirror. It was an elegant, well-chiseled face showing little ravages of the passage of time and history with the exception of a singular frown line cutting deeply between her brows. It was an imperious mark. It reminded her that she wanted things and she was used to getting what she wanted. It did not tell her that she was one of a ruling triumvirate, a person whose will and orders affected whole planets.

With a sigh, the woman broke off her self-examination and quickly began to apply makeup. With fast strokes that betrayed how many times she had done this same routine without change, she finished her cosmetics. A few more strokes and pinnings and her dark, luxurious hair was upswept and captured. She pouted her lips and made a last, desultory examination before turning off the mirror lights and standing. She ran her hands down her flanks, settling her dress into position.

She was as ready to start a revolution as she would ever be.

"You're canny, Pepys," she said to the darkened mirror. "But you've made your moves too late. You should have unleashed Storm sooner."

The stalker in the hallway had been coming to its feet in a fluid move. It stuttered to a halt at the dialogue, then regathered itself and launched.

The in-house cameras recorded only a blur of light, energy too potent for the film to capture well, a levin-bolt of death. When the assassin finished, the body of the woman known familiarly as the Countess collapsed in a heap without ever having been touched. Blood ran from her delicate nostrils and diamond adorned ears and even in death, the imperious frown mark did not relax.

Vandover slid into the privacy booth, well aware of the unhappiness and hostility in the expression of the man waiting for him. He'd left his robes of office at the palace but still wore black as was his habit. The other shifted his bulky weight as Baadluster did so, as if to keep the table squarely between them. Vandover smiled to himself as he noted the unconscious movement.

The other was just past his prime, his black hair amply flecked with yellowish gray, his haircut out of style and becoming unruly. He looked altogether nondescript and Vandover knew the man's look was as affected as his own. "Naylor," he greeted.

Naylor gave a half-grunt in reply and ignored

Baadluster's hand. He examined his own pinkish palm, which contrasted with the richness of his skin, instead. "You heard fast," he finally said, and there was a tone of defeat in his voice.

Baadluster spread his hands. "What point is there in having the WP and the sweepers, if not to know these things quickly? Still, the house had already been cleaned. Security tapes gone. Recordings gone."

"And you want to know what killed her?" Naylor met his glance with a hard, brown one of his own. "We don't know."

But Vandover was already shaking his head. "That's immaterial at this point. The Countess is gone. Without her, you're adrift."

"I came to meet you because you said you had something interesting to say. I won't sit and listen to you gloat."

"I'm not gloating, my friend. I am commiserating with you. Much good work has been done, but there's a great deal more to do."

Suddenly Vandover had Naylor's full attention. "What do you want with me?" the dusky man asked.

The Minister of War said nothing, but his long tapered fingers etched out the secret greeting of the Green Shirts on the tabletop.

Naylor sat very still on his side of the table, long after Baadluster's hand had ceased to move. Then he nervously wet his lips. "How can I trust you?"

"You can't know. Nor do I know if I can trust you. But I would think, in my position, that I have far more to lose, revealing myself to you." Vandover sat back in the booth. Crystal lights from the shabby bar played over them and the booth's noise curtain muffled what passed for music in the background. He watched and waited as the other came to a decision.

Finally, reluctantly, "What do you want from me?"

"What killed her?"

Naylor shrugged. "We think it was sonics, but we're not sure. The tapes don't reveal anything except some sort of energy surge across the film. It's not a beam of any type we're familiar with. Official cause of death is massive brain hemorrhaging. It could even be natural."

"But it wasn't."

"Not as far as we're concerned."

"How will you carry on without her?"

Naylor hesitated again. He took a drink, saying nothing.

Vandover leaned across the table. "What if I were to offer you cohesion instead of chaos?"

Queen Tricatada rattled her chitin with pleasure as General Guthul approached and did obeisance to her. Opening her back casings, she displayed her wings as only a queen might, their luminescent blue splendor casting a glamour over the Thraks bowed before her. Her body thrummed with the need to be mated, and she favored this warrior Thraks above any who might approach her, but this was not the time or place. She folded her ornamental wings back under her carapaces and settled, signaling Guthul that he might rise. She admired his mask as he levered himself upward.

In the clacks, hums, and trills of their voices, she said to him, "It is good to have you back under my wing, Guthul. Neither the leavings nor the matings have been so sweet."

He inclined his head. "Only duty could drive me from your side."

"How goes our interweaving?"

"The ancient enemy is strong and is as unreadable as ever." The warrior Thraks, in spite of his audience with his queen, could not hold his pose. He began to pace from side to side. "Only your vast superiority in egg-laying keeps them at bay."

The queen projected pride and sorrow in her mask, an artistic rendering of two opposite emotions done with such skill that Guthul stopped in his tracks to admire it. The queen's eyes shone. She had not missed that involuntary adulation. She lowered herself to all fours. "My time is short," she said.

As well the warrior Thraks knew. The burden of laying enough eggs to replenish their society was one no female could bear for long—and yet, the shame of their race was that no other fertile female had yet been hatched. When the queen could no longer bear, their race was doomed. And yet their hope lay in the knowledge that surely the more eggs she bore, the greater the chance of finding another fertile layer must be. Thus her sorrow . . . for the more she bore, the shorter her span as her body slowly, inexorably, gave out. Guthul knew that in his lifetime the ancient battle might well be lost, and his race gone.

Tricatada looked up. "How skillfully have you woven our plans?"

"So skillfully that, I believe, our past foe and current ally has no inkling of our true intent. We are a true mating, you and I," Guthul told her.

"The humans believe our forces intertwined, and yet we dominate with less than a third of our corps engaged."

"Only a third?"

Guthul thrilled to hear his queen suck her breath in with pleasure. It stirred him, made him think of things other than war to quicken his pulse. "As you ordered, it has been done."

"And the council backs me in full agreement." Tricatada rattled her carapaces. "They dare not cross me otherwise. I am the only hope."

Unspoken was the threat that she might withhold laying if the council crossed her. It was a ploy she had told Guthul she might use. The Thrakian League was united behind her because it had no choice. No other faction had a fertile queen it might bring forth to unseat her, and it would take nothing less to break her rule now.

The queen stood up again and looked down on him. "But you have not been entirely successful, General."

He brought his mask into humble statement. "No, my queen, I have not. The commander called Storm survived our clumsy attack. But I do not think it likely that he alone can sway the Triad Throne or the Dominion even if he should guess the truth. They are not like us. No one being can encompass the power and authority we do."

Tricatada paused in the process of stroking her flank. "Think you not? I think, my warrior, you had best turn your talents to finding that one known as Colin of the Blue Wheel. Our sources tell us that Pepys is mounting a search and rescue for that one. It will involve Storm. I do not like the implications. The Walkers have impeded our norcite mining long enough. He is bound to, if he has not already, discover that which we do not want known. If Colin is to be found, I want it to be by us."

Guthul bowed. "Yes, my queen." He knew an order when he heard one. Whatever misgivings he had about the assignment, he put them aside.

Tricatada paused. "Try to put K'rok into the detail. The Milot is a capable being and we have found him useful in the past."

"As you command." Guthul stopped. Without seeming to, he changed the projection of his mask slightly, dominating and courageous. He could no longer ignore the scent she had begun to secrete. He had been taken from her side for too long and though no Thraks claimed monogamy, he was her prime mate and thought to remind her of it. "The defense lines have been drawn, my queen. When the Ash-farel fall upon us this time, it will be the foreign bodies who protect us. The human realm from the Outward Bounds to the Dominion to the Triad Throne itself will be sacrificed to ensure your survival. And while they fight and die, the swarm will carry us far beyond their reach. I, Guthul, pledge this to you. We shall triumph."

Tricatada's throaty reply was nearly inaudible, sensually drowned by her call to mating. With a cry of his own, Guthul mounted her, and she spread her wings over the two of them as they answered a more primitive call to the survival of the species.

When Guthul left her, she lay upon her nesting, deep in sleep, exhausted, the musky scent of their mating pervading her chambers. She did not rouse when the chamberlain slipped in to leave the evening meal. It would not have mattered to her even had she been aware, for the chamberlain was a male drone, and drones by their very nature were inferior and inconsequential. The drone did his duties quietly, so as not to awaken the queen. As Thraks go, he was far more graceful than the warriors, unhampered by the almost metallic shielding of their carapaces and chiton.

When he should have left, he paused by the nest of the queen. Her mating scent thrilled him as well. He was insignificant, a nothing, his matings confined to the inconsequential drones of his caste, but he found himself irrevocably aroused by his queen. In an act which would mean nothing less than the annihilation of his familial nest if it were ever discovered, the drone mounted the queen and sated himself on her unconscious body. Tricatada moaned and thrashed in dreamy awareness, for the drone's member was also unhampered by the body armor of a warrior Thraks and pierced her with far more strength. As she responded to his mating, the drone spent himself hastily and withdrew, knowing that he had committed the most heinous sin one of his caste could. In haste he fled the chambers, his mask concealing his shame.

Chapter 17

His life was peeled away from him layer by layer, sometimes poignant and sometimes sweet, like the skin of an onion, but always painful. He hung onto his existence tenaciously, unwilling to let it go no matter how painful. No doubt the Ash-farel observed this about him as much as they did the veinings and ganglia they traced. He had no way of knowing their reaction to his humanness, but their surgical skill he could attest to in that he still lived at all.

Strange to be alive and yet disembodied, to search for comfort and find only more agony, to look for death and see instead the myriad points of his soul that were connected to others. He brushed the consciousness of Jack's armor and then Jack himself, emperors and knaves, and the shadowy glint of Amber's thoughts, nothing he could anchor himself to and yet interwoven strongly throughout himself. He found he could not pray to die, that to let go now would cause a vast unweaving of a pattern he couldn't yet admire. So he clung to the strands of his life and his soul with all the feeble weakness he could muster.

It must have been enough. He slowly became aware that the Ash-farel were putting him back together. The vastly separated stars of his life and thought rushed close and connected again. No longer was he strewn against the dark threshold of his own death.

He awoke to greater pain than he had ever known, to a body that was his and yet not his. The Ash-farel had taken him apart and put him back together. But for all their skill, they had not done it correctly.

Chapter 18

"I heard the emperor was taking appointments for audiences again." A frail, wispy white-haired man stood at the palace viewscreen. He shifted his weight nervously from one foot to the other. "I need to talk with him as soon as possible." His release from the Green Shirt lab kept him on edge, moving, fearful of being found. He'd been told to seek out the Minister of War, but to give his message in person.

An officious looking woman stared back at him. "State your name, Church ranking, and affiliation."

"Church? I—" the being stammered to a halt.

"You're not a Walker?"

"Why, no, I . . . I'm a xenobiologist," the man said, with the shreds of his dignity.

"I'm sorry," the hawk-nosed woman told him. "The audience chambers are being opened to Walkers only."

"But I—"

"I'm sorry," she repeated icily. "Strike negotiations must take precedence. Surely you understand that. Public audiences will be opening once the general strike has been settled."

"I *must* talk with Baadluster," Mierdan in-sisted. "I have something important to tell him that I cannot submit by com line. There must be something you can do—tell him—"

The woman had been seated on-screen. Now she got to her feet, and he knew instantly he'd been pleading with the wrong person as she came out from behind the shelter of her console. Not only was she massive, but the crude cross that vibrated with irritation on her heaving breast identified her as a Walker herself. "I've called for palace security," she told him. "I suggest you leave before they respond."

Mierdan turned and fled. He had no desire to be detained by the World Police. The street beyond the palace gates remained open and quiet. He paused. Having come this far. . . . He turned back, brushing at the front of his rather seedy clothing. His old security clearance had gotten him this far. Despite his reedy stature and frail nerve, he was not inclined to give up this easily. His lab work had been poorly funded and ill-received, but he had information which could change the entire structure of the Thrakian alliance. The rioting over St. Colin's disappearance aside, nothing could be more important than this, but he had to tell the minister face to face. The Thraks had infiltrated Malthen too thoroughly. With the loss of the countess, his benefactors had been thrown into chaotic inaction. Mierdan could wait no longer.

The sound of Thrakian chittering brought him to a halt and then a dash into the greenery bordering the grounds. His skin prickled with fear and he ground his teeth to keep them from chattering and to hold back the bile in his throat. He'd spent too many years as a Thrakian captive to lose his freedom now. He listened to them pass. He caught a little sense of their communication. The Walker situation was being closely watched. But these were warrior Thraks and most of their conversation was of eagerness to fight and wondering when they would be unleashed to do so. Mierdan found the warrior Thraks muscle-bound and dull, single-minded. The only warrior Thraks of any subtlety and guile the man had ever known had been Guthul. Guthul, he sensed, could easily have been a diplomatic Thraks as well.

When the aliens had passed, Mierdan crawled out on stomach and pointed elbows, to see where he had brought himself. He did not recognize the outbuildings or the massive, fire-walled stadium beyond but he knew he had to be near the barracks for the Dominion Knights. To be caught here might well cost him his life, if the Thraks did not get hold of him first. Mierdan scurried back into the foliage.

Voiccs carricd, human voices. The tiny man ducked his face down and hoped that his thatch of now-white hair remained unseen among the greenery.

"That's done, then," growled a coarse voice. "Fitted for th' suit and backed as well as you can be, Commander."

The second voice was milder in tenor but it drew Mierdan's attention immediately. He strained against the impulse to look up, to match gazes with the owner of that voice. "K'rok surprised me."

"I'd give my left nut to know why queenie let him off the hook so's he could go with you, other than to spy."

"Me, too. K'rok has never been wholly loyal to his Thrakian host, but neither can I count on an alliance with him. I'll have Rawlins and Amber with me."

Mierdan edged his chin up over a leafy branch. He could clearly see the two men who spoke and he muffled his shock with a trembling hand. He knew he'd recognized that voice—he could not forget the man who'd saved his life and brought him home alive from Klaktut—but the man had been captured by Pepys as a traitor. What miracle was this?

The Knight's voice cut through his confusion. "I don't want Amber along."

Lassaday brayed in response, then said, "You won't be keepin' that one behind! Not anymore."

"She deserves better, Sarge. Pepys is letting me go after Colin—but I haven't been reinstated and I may not be, regardless of what he says. I'm a traitor and when the emperor has no further use for me, I won't have much of a future."

"You're no deserter, Commander," answered Lassaday with conviction.

Mierdan's mouth hurt from the pressure of his hand across it. He watched the two men continue walking, taking them out of ear and eyeshot. His information was privileged, yet no one would hear him . . . and he could think of no one else who would put it to better use than Commander Storm. Yet Mierdan was confused by the apparent resurrection and by the words "traitor" and "deserter." He brushed hesitation aside and stood up. Leaves tangled in his wispy hair.

A shadow darker than those of tree and limb fell across him. Mierdan looked up and shrank aside

as the massive battle armor dwarfed him. He
could not read what manner of face was behind
the visor as the right gauntlet reached out and engulfed his shoulder.

"...be doing here, little man?"

"Storm," he got out. ...olve dried in his throat. ...must see Commander
Storm."

The gauntlet closed on his shoulder until bone
and cartilage moved in protest and flesh pulped
into bruises. "What say you?"

"I must find Commander Storm!" Mierdan's
voice went falsetto as the gauntlet drew him up
on his toes, dangling in pain. In sudden panic, he
twisted loose, the fabric covering his shoulder
tearing and he sprinted away, darting out of sight
and through the palace gates. The hulking figure
in battle armor looked after him, suit cameras
taking a record of each and every step.

Mierdan reached dubious sanctuary in under-
Malthen and closed his door behind him, panting
with nervous energy. His shoulder twinged with
every breath or movement, yet he could tell from
gingerly testing it that nothing had been broken
or permanently damaged. Those suits were powerful! With only a little more effort from the
wearer, he would have been pulverized.

It was a long time after his heart and pulse
calmed before he moved away from the door and
crossed the shabby room where the Green Shirts
had secreted him and his work. What use they'd
have for him now, he did not know. His whole
world had gone topsy-turvy once again. He did not

Charles Ingrid

know whom to trust. He put no stock in the expediency of politics.

He began to clean up the tiny lab, destroying tapes and disks as he went. His work he worked engraved indelibly in his memory. He worked leave evidence for others to his shoulder or feverishly, heedless of his stomach. When done, of the growing hunger in his stomach. When done, he would destroy the lab and flee, to think about what he knew and decide what it was best to do with the information. He would be a hunted man, not only by the Green Shirts who would think he had betrayed them, but by the Thraks who wanted him back desperately. He would have to plan well.

Mierdan never heard his door being forced, but when the overhead lights blacked out, he turned to look—and saw the colossal being occupying the building, eclipsing the lights with its armored bulk.

The being reached up and took off its helmet. The biologist saw the furred and ursine face of a Milot. His heart sank. He knew of only one Milot who served both the Thrakian League and the Dominion Knights.

The being smiled widely, fangs glinting. "I be following you, little man. Now what is being so important you must talk to Commander Storm?"

His tongue clove to the roof of his mouth. Mierdan backed away, blinking frantically. The debris underfoot crunched. "I—I have information for him," he finally managed.

"Only for Jack?" the Milot swung about, looking the building over. He hunkered down in the battle armor, bringing his massive face level with Mierdan's. "Let's not be fooling one another, little

man. I be K'rok and you be Mierdan. My queen
wants you back very badly."

"I—I'm not property! I'm a f–free man!"

"And a frightened one." The Milot did not move.
"I be telling you what few know. I also am free,
though my queen would have my head and the
grubs would feed off my body if she be knowing I
say this. You came to find Storm. He is in great
trouble now. But tell me your message and I will
be giving it to him."

"And then you'll go?"

K'rok nodded his shaggy head affirmatively.

Mierdan stood in frightened shock a moment
longer. Then, as K'rok's gauntleted hand came up,
the pain of his shoulder decided him. The words
bolted out of him. "It's about the norcite. Storm
knows a little—he knows I've been working on the
problem. You tell him. I lived among the Thraks.
The grubs and drones are different from the others. The carapaces, the chiton, are much softer
and flexible. I know why the Thraks covet the norcite. For a while we thought they might use a solution to coat themselves, like enamel, but that's
not it. But Jack's old armor is coated with norcite
and there were times when he was almost sure
Thraks couldn't see him. Well, they could, but
didn't."

"Slow down," K'rok growled.

Mierdan took a gulping breath. Then, "It's like
this. They grind the ore to powder and ingest it.
That greatly strengthens the armor. The lesser
castes don't do it—it's not necessary. So when
norcite is sensed in the composition of another—
the Thraks don't see the way we do—they think
they're sensing another Thraks. But now they

know the enemy is using norcite, too, so they take that into account. But what they don't know is that norcite is affecting them adversely. Tell Jack norcite is the answer." Mierdan slowed to a halt. He clouded his last words deliberately, unwilling to give the Milot all his information. But Storm was savvy and would make the connection. The little man gave a quivery smile in relief.

"And that is being all?"

"Yes. Can you remember that?"

"Oh, yes." The Milot rose and shook himself. The Flexalinks gave a shimmering dance in the lights. "I be remembering all of this very well. And you?"

"I destroyed my records."

"Good." The Milot replaced his helmet. "I am sorry, little man." He reached out. Mierdan had a second to let out a terrified squeak, then his head cracked audibly and he went limp in K'rok's hands. He held the body until he was sure death had come, then he lowered it gently to the lab floor. The armor obscured the emotion in his voice. "No one is being entirely free," he said. "They would hound you to your death. Now you are being beyond them." With deliberate grace, he stepped over the body and left the shabby laboratory.

Chapter 19

Pepys shrugged on his red and gold threaded robes with great difficulty. The floor to ceiling com screen was filled with the visage of his caller and he had ordered his dressers to leave so that he might speak in private. The Thrakian queen looked at him with an amused glint in her faceted eyes. He wondered if she thought he put on body armor and found it amusing. His hair crackled in annoyance as he ran a hand through it.

"I do not threaten well, if at all," he told her. There was a long pause for transmittal during which he changed his slippers for dress boots.

Then, "It is not a threat. It is a promise. We have invested much in our alliance. You are on the brink of . . . internal warfare. We intend to step in before the Dominion decides that it has the option to do the same."

Fury ignited in him, burning deep in his stomach like a suddenly flaring ember. He fisted his hand. "I will declare the alliance at an end."

Could a Thraks laugh? Her gloriously colored blue and gold chitin appeared to shake. "How, Pepys? We are entangled among you. Your armor is our armor—to separate us will leave us both exposed to the Ash-farel. Put your nest in order before you tear us all down. We shall be close, waiting." Tricatada tilted her head. Her throat leather fluttered, and her mask closed into an expression of beauty and command. The screen went gray.

Pepys fastened his overrobes with shaking hands. The Dominion was to be his and his alone. Even if Storm somehow managed to find Colin and return with him, forcing Pepys to be true to his word and step down, the Dominion awaited him. Tricatada hinted at betrayal and conquest under the cloak of martial law. He would find a way to stave her off. Today's audience was only the first in a series of steps. Much depended on Storm and if the mind block Pepys had instituted was finally wearing off, he would be the weapon Pepys needed—when Storm was out of Vandover's range.

Pepys finished his outfitting. *I'll give you your saint, friend, and a kingdom beyond that. Pray God you'll never have to head it.* With a shrug, he signaled for his ministers and went out to meet the humble Walkers who threatened to topple his reign.

Jack woke with the bitter taste of *mordil* still on his tongue, the empty vial clenched in his hand. He released his grip gingerly and let the vial drop. He had beaten the night. His dreams and memories were still his own this morning. With a powerful stretch, he eased his muscles into waking and got up. His dress uniform hung on a stretcher, reminding him that Pepys was putting him on display.

His imprint slipped over him from time to time,

leaving him with annoying gaps of time, and nighttime was the worst. There were other drugs he could use to sleep, but *mordil* was the least destructive. It was worth it if he could face himself in the mirror and remember his family. The blackouts worried him less and less—the memories always came back. There was only the worry that he might commit a fatal mistake with Pepys or Vandover—and he was more likely to do that as himself, than as his imprint. He was not supposed to remember the years of intrigue and bad faith.

Nor was he expected to remember that Pepys had promised to step down if he found Colin. With a wry smile, Jack made his way to the refresher. As he passed through the apartment, he caught a bare hint of perfume and stopped to inhale it.

Had Amber been here again while he slept? He cast about, trying to catch the perfume again, wondering if he'd only imagined it. Then, having grasped nothing, he continued to the refresher. He had not seen Amber for several days, though Lassaday told him she'd come in for a suit fitting. He would arouse suspicion if he sought her out.

He stepped into the shower and let it beat down on his neck and shoulders, hammering out tense muscles. He walked a razor's edge with Amber's life and knew it, and did not know how to tell her he knew it. There were too many others with too much at stake listening to every word he might say to her. He could only hope that Amber could take care of herself, as she always had. He stood in the shower until the fog in the stall enveloped him.

Vandover and Pepys wanted a tame act they

could trot before the Walkers to placate them. Jack did not know the Walker organization well save for Colin, Jonathan, and Denaro, and Colin's harsh-faced secretary, Margaret—but he knew about the turmoil within the organization and that Colin's amenable philosophy had always been in danger. The Walkers would not settle for the crumbs Pepys was hoping to toss them. Jack wanted to be there, if for no other reason than that. The order had been, no suits. If Jack had been commanding, it would have been, no Thraks. Pepys would be doing well to keep the lid on.

This would be Jack's resurrection. The Triad Throne had declared him dead and buried, after all, months before tracking him down and bringing him back as a traitor and deserter. It wouldn't due to be late.

Anticipating action at last, after weeks of imprisonment, he put his dress uniform on.

Amber chose a dress that would not reveal her bruises, though her chapped and swollen lips she would have to disguise. She watched herself as she crossed the room to finish dressing. She moved like a cheap and crudely assembled doll. Amber paused, caught in the mesh of her own stare and the thoughts it precipitated.

She should tell Jack. She knew the gentlemanly creed that was at the core of the man she'd loved—it was still there. The imprint had probably made him stronger than ever. Jack would kill Vandover, remembering her or not. But there would be retribution and she would never ask Jack to give his life up for her justice. And there was always the chance that Jack would not be fast enough to kill Baadluster before he ordered her to kill Jack.

She smeared her thumb over her lips, harshly, savagely, as if assessing how much pain remained in them. It was just her flesh, after all. Just flesh. Amber turned away then, unable to meet the look in her own eyes. Vandover had spilled his foul, black seed in her mind as well and she could feel it growing there. He had chains for her very thoughts—and would not hesitate to use them.

She finished her hair and makeup quickly, unable to meet the accusation in her eyes. She'd let him do it. But no, she'd fought and been beaten. There was nothing she could have done. Was there? *Was there?*

A sound at her door kept the tears from welling in her eyes. She signaled it open and stood quickly, expecting to see Jack standing there, ready to escort her to the audience, and she secured the last of her knives in her gloves. "Jack, you're early—" Her words ground to a halt as Baadluster filled the portal.

He wore slate today, and a short overrobe that showed his whippet lean body. He looked, she thought, like one of the dark poisonous blades she had just hidden in her wrist sheath. He showed his teeth in a smile. "Milady," he said, in that tone that oozed other meanings into what he said. *Whore,* she thought. *He always means whore when he says that ... and now he is right.* "You were expecting someone else?"

"Old habits die hard," Amber bit off. "What do you want?" She kept distance between them.

"Only the pleasure of your accompanying me to the hall. Pepys will be seated shortly."

"I can find my way there alone."

"Of a surety. But there is something I wish to say to you first." And he halved the distance.

Her pulse skidded. "I've already done a job for you."

"Amber, Amber. You don't think I wasted all that money and those years in training for one name and one name alone, do you? That was just a demonstration for you and some of my opponents. A little warning that disobedience is futile." His lips thinned. "Come here, Amber."

Nausea rocked her stomach. She stepped toward him. The room had gone suddenly cold. "Not Jack," she protested.

"No, no. Not Jack. Jack has to find St. Colin and, if we're very lucky, bring home the secrets of the Ash-farel." He crooked his finger. "Closer, milady. I know your aversion to security systems and that you have this room well sealed, but some things are meant to be whispered."

The hall looked resplendent. Laser holograms filled the domed roof with a silvery net of planets and stars depicting the worlds that mankind had touched. Banners rippled in the current of an unseen breeze. Voices filled the air, muted and multitudinous. Anyone and everyone who could possibly gain entrance had. They had not minded the wait since early dawn nor the shuffle through the weapons net for clearance nor even the near stifling crowding of the audience floor. All they had to do was stretch their necks and look upward, where the stars roamed freely above them.

A hush fell over the crowd as Pepys entered from the private chambers to the rear and took his place on the stage throne. A small, golden android came to the fore and cried out, "Oyez, oyez, his right honorable majesty, Emperor Pepys, sits in court to address the suits and grievances being brought before him. All hail Emperor Pepys."

As the crowd responded, the Minister of War emerged and took his shadowy place to the right of the throne. Pepys turned and their gazes met. Vandover had been late, too late to discuss last minute details in the private chambers, so late that Pepys had even wondered if his minister would be attending him. As the emperor studied him now, he saw a few blonde hairs trailing upon the minister's black vest. His attention immediately flicked back to the hall, but he could not see Amber among the throng. He did see Jack, to the left, his dress uniform bare of rank and honor, at attention.

Worriedly, Pepys turned his focus back to the ceremony at hand. He knew Baadluster intended to dispose of the girl soon. Looking at the crush of people before the dais, he wondered how and when Vandover would terminate her. An assassin could move through such a crowd easily. He got to his feet. The immense hall full of people fell to a hush.

"Good people. This is the first time the audience hall has been open since the known disappearance of Colin of the Blue Wheel, my friend and adviser, as well as the prelate of the Walker religion. Many of you have come to petition me to seek for him, unaware of the exhaustive search we have been conducting in conjunction with the Dominion and the Thrakian League. While his whereabouts are not certain, we do have some idea of where he intended to go when he disappeared.

It is my sad duty to inform you that he is not lost, he has been taken, in all probability, by the Ash-farel." Pepys paused dramatically, the vidscreens about the hall reflecting the vivid color of his green eyes in close-up. He listened to the gasps and cries of his distressed audience. His gaze lingered on the stern visage of Margaret, Colin's longtime secretary, who had helped him arrange this event. She stood in the cordoned off area before the platform along with others—Dominion senators, Walker ministers, ambassadors—who had specific permission to question him along with the different reporters and recorders. She showed no surprise on her hawklike face. He was only confirming what she was already privy to.

"I do not know why Colin placed himself in such jeopardy. It is our feeling that he hoped to treat with an enemy that has proven itself inscrutable as well as invincible. That would have been much like my old friend, to place the common good before his own welfare. But the fact remains that he is needed and wanted here, and if we can return him, we will!" Another pause, this one heralded by shouts and ovations. As he looked around, gauging the reaction, he saw Amber, in an emerald dress echoing the color of his eyes, edging closer. As if in response, Jack's head turned as well, to watch her.

There was a spate of questions being shouted at him from the cordoned off section. He put his hands out palms up to quiet them. "Military response," he said, "would prove futile. Our intelligence sources have not yet been able to pinpoint the sectors of space our enemy calls home. We cannot predict when or from where they will attack. We do feel that they have the capabilities to mount massive warships and leave them cruising at large, to take whatever opportunity they can to strike at us. This random pattern increases their invincibility as well as our vulnerability."

Pepys halted. He reached for the goblet on the side table and took a sip of water to clear his drying throat. Vandover looked up at him through flat black eyes and smiled bleakly. The emperor nodded at him.

"My capable Minister of War, Vandover Baad-luster, however, has defended us most ably. Within our alliance, we have begun to mount a defensive line, a stellar demarcation and thus far, we have been able to turn the Ash-farel away along that front." *Hopeful lies*, Pepys thought, *but no one here with the information or the authority to contradict him.*

"As for Colin, myself and my advisers have concluded that a small, handpicked unit will be the most effective way to search for him. To that end, I have conducted a search of my own for the man to lead that unit. You have all heard the rumors and now it is time to set them to rest.

About a year and a half ago, it was my sad duty to officiate at a funeral for an officer who had given much to our throne. Imagine my shock when information came to me indicating that this officer had not died, his body unrecoverable on a far-away world, but had instead deserted his command. We verified our intelligences and went in search of this officer. I brought him back with me for the sole purpose of locating Colin of the Blue

Wheel and vindicating his desertion." Pepys looked to Jack and found Jack's attention already upon him. The rock steadiness of the man unnerved Pepys slightly. What confidence, to stand among a crowd which might well stone him to death for his betrayal. He motioned for Jack to join him on the dais.

There was a murmur of unrest, growing in volume, as Jack mounted the stage and came to parade rest to Pepys' left. "Ladies and gentleman, the last living Knight of the Sand Wars, Commander Jack Storm."

Pepys waited quietly through the commotion that followed, listening to the shouts and demands and half-scattered applause, timing his remarks to follow. After a few moments, he signaled his speaker and held up his hands for silence as the android called for it.

"Commander Storm is no stranger to controversy," Pepys said. "But I have found in him a man who has always done as he believes is his duty. He has undertaken trials for me that would have broken a lesser officer. His courage and ability to think independently under fire are qualities that cannot be forced upon a man. He is the only officer I can think of who has a chance of going after Colin and bringing him home, if he is still alive."

"He has asked me for this opportunity to vindicate himself against the charges of deserter and traitor." Pepys hesitated. "I have decided to give him this chance. Finding St. Colin is a challenge, and I have the man to meet it." He stepped back, leaving Jack alone to face the audience. "Ladies and gentleman, I give you Commander Storm." He returned to his throne.

There was a stunned silence, then a sudden clamor as reporters pressed close to hurl their questions at him. Jack did not turn to look after Pepys. He had been half-expecting such drama from the emperor. He pointed at an individual and prepared to field his question.

"Commander Storm, why did you leave your post? Was it cowardice?"

The vidscreens posted about the hall seemed to echo the question in the sudden silence. Jack wet his lips. He saw Amber edge into the cordoned area and stand at Margaret's elbow. The Walker secretary scarcely seemed to notice her.

He looked out. "Rather than answer individual questions, I would like to make a statement at this time. I left my command under Pepys because I felt the Thrakian alliance had compromised the security of the Dominion and the Triad Throne. I was wrong to do so. It was not my duty to question the decision." Jack paused again. He could feel Baadluster's stare on him, as well as that of Pepys. They had discussed this position with him and he did not know whether he betrayed his true self or not. "I took it upon myself to search out the nature of this new enemy, the Ash-farel. Emperor Pepys has taken this into account, along with my service record, and decided that I would be the best man to undertake this assignment. I'm not sure he's right—but I welcome the opportunity to prove myself a Knight worthy of the rank. Thank you."

Furor broke out as he stepped back to flank Pepys. The emperor gave him a bemused smile.

Baadluster remained expressionless. Out of range of the speaker, Pepys said softly, "Now I know why I picked you for the job."

But the audience was not pleased. Accusations and questions were hurled at them until Jack was forced to step forward and say, "No comment." His silence drove them to further displays of their displeasure until Margaret approached the edge of the platform. Then the hall fell quiet.

"We will not," she said, and the speaker carried her firm voice to the farthest corners of the chamber, "be placated by you. Your promises are as empty as most of the bellies on Malthen. You are an emperor who refuses to hear or represent our will and then tries to foist a traitor on us as a savior. It's not good enough and we won't stand for it. You no longer have a mandate to rule us, Pepys."

Jack searched the crowd and saw his fellow Knights moving quietly forward to form a bastion between the platform and the audience.

Pepys stood again. "We are at war with an enemy that threatens to destroy us utterly. We cannot win that war if we are divided against ourselves!"

"That is a choice you've made." Margaret pointed at him. She looked like a long-ago prophetess. "We are not divided against *you*."

The aureole of his frizzed red hair wavered as he moved to the very edge of the dais to meet the Walker's tall, commanding figure. "You threaten civil war. Officers, remove this woman."

Jack looked at Amber, standing in Margaret's wake. Vandover said something inaudible, and

Amber's attention snapped toward him. Then, with a tiny frown, she turned her gaze on Pepys.

The emperor let out a sharp cry. He swayed as the crowd, sensing something was wrong, began to scream.

Only Jack was close enough to catch him as the man went down.

Chapter 20

Other forces were in motion even before Jack reached for his falling sovereign. He could see the ripple of movement throughout the immense hall. As he put out his arms to catch Pepys, he called out sharply. "Amber! Get clear!"

Vandover seemed like a puff of charcoal smoke as he turned and bolted for the exit behind the dais. Pepys hit Jack's embrace. Ribbons of crimson streamed from his ears and nose and one vermilion drop from his eye etched a tearlike path down his cheek. Amid the screams and jostling, Jack could hear the Knights and then the WP clearing the room, but his keen ears heard more— the sound of armed conflict in the hallways.

K'rok and his Thraks emerged at the portal, his armor streaked with smoke stains. The Thrakian Knights wore Enduros rather than the full battle armor, though they did have modified suits. The bracers and adapted headgear they wore now made them look like some kind of mutated cyborg. The immense Milot plowed to a halt.

"See this area is being secured," he ordered. The Thraks fanned out, pushing the last of the crowd out, oblivious to the hysteria around them.

Pepys moaned as Jack lowered him carefully to the dais. K'rok loomed over them.

"Medical is en route, but the palace is being overrun. The Walkers came with an army, eh. What happened?"

"I don't know." Jack checked the emperor's pulse. It was slow and erratic, but the man still breathed laboriously. He pulled aside the heavy imperial robes to give what ease he could. "He just collapsed." He heard something at his back and saw Amber standing there. "Are you all right?"

"Yes. Who would have thought Margaret could set off a revolution?"

"More likely she just gave a signal." He turned his attention back to the emperor. The man's hand was slack in his and the flesh was growing cooler by the moment. "K'rok, where's medical?"

The Milot swiveled. "The corridors up here have been sealed off. They're fighting their way through. Jack, I am getting reports that the airports and space berths have been taken."

"The streets of Malthen are running with blood," Amber said tonelessly. Jack turned quickly to her but could read nothing in her expression.

"Who's in control?"

"For the moment," Vandover said smoothly, as he returned from the secured privacy chambers to the stage's rear, "it appears no one is. I'm in charge as long as the emperor is incapacitated, but the Triad Throne is under siege." He looked at Amber and Jack. "I've just received word that the Thrakian League is closing in. They state that, as allies, they have no choice but to impose martial law in Pepys' name."

"Legal invasion," Jack muttered. He stared down at the man on the dais who fought for every breath. "You son of a bitch."

"Jack," said Amber softly, warningly.

He looked up and saw K'rok with his gauntlets leveled on him. Jack smiled. "Don't worry. He's either going to make it or not without my help."

The Milot in battle armor shifted away. By the time he reached the hall's doors, he was in full stride, the floor ringing under every strike of the Flexalink boots. As he reached the corridor, fire flash illuminated him for a moment as eerily as if he'd been struck by lightning. The boom and yells and noise of return fire echoed in the empty hall.

Then K'rok reappeared, medical teams streaming in in his wake. Jack let go of Pepys' cool hand and stood back to let them do their work.

Amber had changed from her gown to a jumpsuit of somber brown, a subtle resonance of the color of her eyes. She stood in the hospital wing, chewing a ragged edge of nail off one fingertip. She looked over at Jack. "If you were the man you're supposed to be," she said, "this wouldn't have happened."

"I'm not responsible for an aneurysm."

"No. Of course not." She looked smartly away.

Jack felt the edge of her scorn and anger. He also felt certain that he had given himself away before Vandover in the heat of the moment, but the minister had said little to him once Pepys had gotten out of surgery, the bleeding halted and his condition stabilized. The Triad Throne was under attack within and without and Baadluster had no time for him. Jack's gaze ran over the obsidite walls. He loathed infirmaries, spent as little time in them as possible and yet it seemed as if recently all his days had been spent here. He paced away from Amber. It suddenly seemed necessary to be somewhere, anywhere, else.

With no access to the port where the worst fighting was centered, it would be impossible to get off-planet. Intelligence reports seemed to indicate that even Walker factions were splintered—and getting off world to find Colin would depend on who had control of the port. The Thraks' heaviest concentration was being directed there and Vandover's latest reports seemed to indicate the aliens were gaining ground. But the port was built like a fort, made to withstand the backlash of spacing vehicles . . . squat and solid, damn near unconquerable. It would be a long battle.

Colin was running out of time. Jack could not wait for the tide to turn in a long, drawn out civil war. He had to get off-planet and get off now. He sensed it in every fiber of his being. In all probability, Pepys and Baadluster, too, were playing a game of power far beyond his expectations. The resulting struggles would leave the worlds of mankind open to the Ash-farel. Nothing would survive.

What had been a personal quest for truth and friendship now became something more, a responsibility he was not sure he could shoulder, but knew he had to try.

The care unit door opened and a nurse came through, looking for Jack. He saw Amber drop back fluidly, one hand going to her opposite wrist, as she took up a lethal stance just behind the nurse's shoulder. He had only a split second to wonder what she was doing when the frowning nurse spoke.

"Are you Commander Storm?"

"Yes."

"Good. He's conscious though not entirely lucid, but he refuses to rest until he's spoken with you." The technician hesitated. "Understand that the hemorrhaging has had strokelike aftereffects. He's difficult to understand and he's very weak."

Amber had relaxed her stance. "But he is alive," she asked softly.

"Oh, yes. Very much so." The nurse blocked Amber as she started to follow after Jack. "I'm sorry. Just the commander right now. He's too weak to have visitors."

Amber made a wry face at Jack and let him pass.

The emperor looked like a crumpled up version of himself, the crèche and tubing obscuring all of his body except for his face and hair. When Jack bent near to speak to the man, he noticed for the first time streaks of gray among the fiery red, and that the electricity had gone, leaving the fine strands limp upon the pillow bracing his head. His face had gone slack, and the left side was drawn and twisted, letting drool escape from the corner of his mouth. Jack leaned close, feeling mixed emotions, as he came to the fallen emperor's side.

Pepys' eyes flew open. He stared for a moment, unseeing, then focused on Jack. "Storm," he said, and his mouth and tongue seemed incapable of speaking. Then, with visible effort, he repeated Jack's name.

"Yes."

"What is happening. They won't tell me." Each word took a lifetime. Each breath was a pant.

Jack put his hand on Pepys' shoulder to calm him. "The Thraks have pulled in."

"Shit." The emperor closed his eyes briefly. He seemed to drift, then he opened them and looked back at Jack. "You must remember who you are. Take command from K'rok. Use the Knights. Fight your way out. Fight the Thraks and find Colin." Spent, the man lapsed into pants. Jack waited until his breathing eased.

He smiled briefly. "Is that an order?"

"It . . . is."

"I owe you no allegiance, highness. I swore my oath elsewhere. But I will find Colin and then we'll come to terms with who is to sit the Triad Throne."

Pepys' eyes widened, then he nodded wearily, and gave a shuffling laugh. "I . . . should have known," he said.

"You should have." Jack straightened. "And you never had to order me to fight Thraks."

Amber was not waiting for him when he left the care unit. The halls of the palace had been cleared of the insurgents, but the obsidite walls showed the scarring of the battle as he made his way past them. Rawlins was waiting for him at the barracks.

He saluted him. "Captain. Emperor Pepys has reinstated me and given me orders that nothing, repeat, *nothing* is to stand in the way of completing our mission."

The fair-haired officer snapped off a return salute. "I'm waiting for orders, sir."

* * *

Amber found Vandover in the war room, surrounded by a com net not unlike the sophisticated
one Pepys used. Nervously, she combed her hair
away from the side of her face as she waited for
his attention.

Finally, Vandover swung about in his chair to
glare at her. "You failed," he said flatly.

She had not known who her target had been until he'd said that final word from the dais, speaking an edict of death. But she could no more have
halted her execution of the act than stopped
breathing. Jack had thrown her off when he'd ordered her to get out of harm's way, but by then
she was certain the damage had been done to
Pepys as she'd seen him collapse in Jack's arms.
She gave Baadluster a humorless laugh. "I did my
best."

"That I doubt. But the fact remains that it may
be good enough. He is incapacitated. I sit where I
wish to sit. And no one is the wiser that it was not
a natural occurrence."

Amber did not counter him. She'd overheard the
technicians talking while Jack was in with Pepys.
The aneurysm had not shown on the emperor's
scans during his annual physical and there was
some suspicion. But nothing could be proved. She
kept her silence.

Vandover gestured. "Jack is giving orders. I'm
anticipating that the search for St. Colin will still
be launched. You, my dear, are among the volunteers. Hadn't you better ready yourself?"

Her nerve broke and she quailed inwardly. She
could feel her skin go pale. "Don't make me go
with him."

Vandover's lips tightened. "Milady, you promised him. And me."

The minister would trigger her against Jack. She knew it. She shut her eyes tightly. "I'll do anything," she said. The words stuck in her throat. Vandover made no response and she wondered if he had heard, so she repeated herself. "Anything. But don't make me go with Jack."

The lank and ugly man threw his head back to laugh. When he finished, he smiled coldly at her. "Amber, you keep underestimating yourself. You have a great deal of work yet to do for me. I need Jack alive and you're the best way I have of keeping him safe. Now go get ready."

Almost out of reach of the man, she turned to flee. He caught her wrist at the last second and pulled her roughly to him. The wires and cables of the com net twisted about her, biting at her bare arms.

"And you should remember that I enjoy what I take much more than what I am given," he told her as he felt himself growing hard.

She tried not to struggle, but could not help it as he began to punish her flesh for her disobedience.

Chapter 21

"And those are the options as I see it," Jack said quietly to the people assembled before him. The barracks fell silent. He put a hand to his forehead and wiped the sweat off. The Malthen season was blazingly hot. The air conditioners were failing, as warfare affected all of the utility services where guerrilla action took its toll. The central wings of the palace had backup solars and generators, of course, but the barracks lay on the outer grounds. He had recircuited some of his available power to create white noise barriers and sound buffers to override the emperor's security equipment. Even as he wiped his hand on his trousers to dry it, the machinery sputtered and the lukewarm air circulating shut off.

"Jeez-a-mighty," Lassaday said, getting to his feet. "I'm going to have t'kick a door open, Commander."

"Not just yet, Sergeant," Jack told him. His mind wavered. Was he going to lose it again, just when he needed to be most steady? He could still achieve what he had to, but this one step forward, two steps backward progress would hinder dangerously what he had to attend to now. "Are we agreed on this? There'll be no coming back if we don't succeed in what we set out to do." He did not need to add that there might be nothing to come back to. If the Thraks broke the backs of the remaining Knights and Pepys' troops, Malthen might well become *sand*. If not, the resultant destruction would bring the world shields down, leaving them vulnerable to the Ash-farel.

"What about Pepys?" Rawlins said, a glint deep in his blue eyes.

"Stabilized. Baadluster has taken over for him. There's no knowing which way the wind lies with that one yet." Jack felt sweat trickling through his scalp and down the back of his neck. The room was becoming stifling.

Lassaday leaned against the wall. "We're agreed, sir."

"Whatever it takes," Rawlins seconded.

Jack took a deep breath. He did not like pitting Walker against Walker, but it was the only way he could gain access to the port berths. The militant faction remained firmly entrenched. Only their brethren could safely approach though it was unlikely they could talk their brothers in arms into relinquishing the port. But he didn't need that. All he needed was a shield to get them that far.

From there, he had his own methods of persuasion. There was only one Walker he knew who could face a battle suit, and he was daring Jack to come get him . . . off-planet.

"All right, then. Sarge, get some air in here."

Lassaday, his bronzed pate gleaming with sweat, keyed the door open. It began to slide, then ground to a halt with a dull whine. A huge, shaggy booted leg kicked it off its tracks.

K'rok leaned in. He grinned hugely. "I be left out of the meeting, eh, Jack?" A detail of Thraks filled the background behind him.

K'rok had gotten cool air piped in. He sat, massively conquering one of Jack's chairs, clad in Enduro bracers and a modified jumpsuit for modesty's sake, his hair and bulk armoring him effectively. The musky and rancid oil smell of him filled Jack's quarters.

"Finding Colin be one of the critical factors of our fate, Jack," the Milot said solemnly. "We cannot turn away from it. I am being here because of my masters—and also because I want to be." He leaned across the table separating the two of them. "Milos is losing *sand.*"

"What?"

K'rok leaned back cagily. "I will not say it a second time. You be hearing me, my friend."

"It's failing?"

"Yes. My homeland is too tough to be defeated. I am too tough to be defeated."

Jack sat back in his chair eyeing his fellow commander. He knew that K'rok was only the most visible of a small community of Milots who had survived the desecration of their homeworld. He also knew that K'rok had grown sons and daughters—and dreams of someday going back. Now that someday was a concrete possibility. If *sand* failed, the Thraks would leave. Milos could be terraformed. K'rok might never live to see the day, but his children could. An officer of the Thrakian League would never never hope to see such a day, but he knew K'rok survived for it. The Milot was the same as telling him of his divided loyalties.

But that meant Jack couldn't trust him completely either and K'rok seemed unaware of the paradox he presented Storm.

K'rok's headset was down around his neck, but he wore an abstracted look as if listening to it now and again. He clenched his bulky hand now. "We are out of time, friend Jack." He got to his feet and signaled the Thrakian officers waiting just outside the sound curtain shielding Jack's doorway. "A massive attack is being launched. It appears that the insurgents are calling for Pepys' head."

Jack got up hastily. He reached for the pack he intended to take off world with him. "We'd better suit up," he said. "And it's time to decide who the real enemy is."

K'rok responded with a growling laugh. As he passed through the brace of guards, he moved with a speed that belied his bulk and laid the two Thraks out. Jack dealt a mercy blow to one while K'rok handled the second. Then he stood.

"Casualties of the rebellion, eh?"

"Looks like. How many Thraks are in the barracks?"

"Close to a hundred."

"May I suggest, Commander, that you put them to the fore of our defense against the assault coming in?"

"Good idea."

Jack reshouldered his pack. "We will take the shop and secure it, and work our way back to the palace. Then we work our way out until we meet the front."

* * *

With stiff, jerky movements, Amber gathered up her belongings and packed them. Her arms felt as though they had been pulled from their sockets and her ribs protested the new bruises laid over the old. But he had not taken her again—she'd struggled vigorously enough that he'd been forced to let her go, or risk damaging his communication equipment. Vandover had not seemed to mind it as she fled from him. He took more joy from the pain than from the sex.

But she could no longer flee his thoughts. They followed her, smoldering, like the guttering flame of a trash dump fire, rancid and smutty, choking her own thoughts down. As if he'd realized that she was aware of his invasion, there was an echoing, guttural laugh and he was gone.

Amber staggered to a chair. She sat, holding her face in her hands, trying to breathe. Clean air, clean lungs, clean thought. With a shudder, she looked up. He *would* make her kill Jack, she had no doubt of that. But when? When would he be done with the two of them? Could she break Vandover's hold over her? She wouldn't even hear the words when he whispered them in her ear—how could she turn them away?

She dashed away the tears that threatened to spill. Tears would not help. She had asked for this, in a way. She had wanted to be deadly, to be lethal again. Now she was. How could she face Jack this way? How could she reach out to him? He would never be able to love her again.

She clenched her fist. The sinews on her thin but powerful wrist stood out. She stared at it. The delicate skin on the inside of her wrist was bare where most denizens of Malthen wore a microchip just under the surface. She did not carry a computer ident and never would. She had fought to stay free of that chain. She raised her fist higher.

The first thing she had to do was keep Jack alive. Then she would worry about the rest.

A klaxon broke the stream of her thoughts. In the corner of her tiny room, the com came on. "General alert. Repeat, this is a general alert. We are under attack."

Muttering a street slang curse from the roughest part of under-Malthen, Amber grabbed her kit and ran.

The rebels broke through before they could establish a line. Jack felt good in his suit, despite its bulk and the room he had inside of it, a good soldier wore his armor like a second skin. Point a gauntlet and fire. Or shoulder the field pack and laser cannon. He was a human tank, damn near invincible—but not quite invincible enough.

For the first time in his fighting life, he looked out across a field of enemy who were not the enemy, though they had brought the battle to him. They were flesh he did not want to see burned or blasted. They were fighting for something he might well be fighting for himself, except that he had been trapped on this side.

K'rok bellowed over the com, "Keep it defensive!" He strode over the outer perimeter like some massive mountain come to the aid of the emperor. "Link together and hold the front!"

There would be no holding of this front without killing. Jack swung about. "Rawlins!"

"Yessir."

"Is the shop clear?"

"Shut down and shielded, sir."

The equipment not in use would remain safe—and out of insurgent hands. Jack shrugged into his shoulder pads, feeling the leads and wires clipped to his bare torso pinch more tightly in reaction. If necessary, they could all fall back to the main wing of the palace and shield there as well—but it would only be a matter of time before they would have to come out for supplies. It was not a strategic position one wanted to be in.

He had no time for further thought as his front cameras and grid showed him incoming rebels. With screams that broke into static over his sensors, the enemy charged. He fired over their heads. He brought down trees in their path, exploded ditches before their feet . . . and, in the end, he shot a few.

The numbers were overwhelming. He caught sight of K'rok's suit. "We're going to be up to our helmets in bodies," he said.

A heavy grunt answered. Then K'rok said, "There is always being plan two, Jack."

Plan two might well prove to be the lesser of two evils. "All right," Jack told him.

"Good. Listen up, this is being Commander K'rok. Fall back!"

Pepys slowly became aware that someone sat on the edge of his medical crèche. His head ached, and one eye seemed out of focus—the barely seen visitor took a damp cloth and wiped it for him.

"Thank you," he said, and found his voice in a hot, hoarse whisper, barely audible.

"Don't mention it."

The emperor smiled. "I cannot see you well, Amber, but my hearing is fine."

"Yeah, well, it's about all you've got going for you. Take your ice chips."

Pepys took a cup being folded into his hand—weak, he was so incredibly weak—and the crèche shifted so that he could sit up. He tapped a few chips into his mouth, felt a couple skid off his chin, and tried to suck on the remaining cold miracles. Their refreshing strength trickled down his throat. His eye cleared a little, as well.

Amber was watching the corridor outside the care unit.

"What's happening?"

"Someone started a civil war. I think it was a religious fanatic and a half-assed emperor."

Pepys started to laugh, found himself choking and at her mercy as she helped him to spit up the dust clogging his throat. He sat back, hands shaking as he feebly tried to straighten his covers. "I know that," he said, a little peevishly. "What's happening now?"

"The hospital wing is the most secure part of the palace. We're about to be up to our neck in WP and battle armor."

He tried to think. It eluded him for a moment, then he grasped that they were mounting a last ditch stand and hold effort. "My God." He gasped. "Has it come to that?"

"For the moment." Amber faced him. He thought she looked both tough and beautiful. "Got any ideas?"

"None." He lay back and took a deep breath. He hurt all over, and was strangely numb in places he shouldn't be. "Where are the nurses?"

"Most of your palace staff fled along with your psychics, valets, cooks and maids, and medical staff. But you still have your Knights." She gave him a crooked grin.

"Yes. I would, wouldn't I." No matter what he had done to Storm, the man had stayed with him, kept there by his own brand of ethics. "Where's Vandover?"

"He's deploying the WP officers. He's been running your show, you know."

"I know, my dear. I know." Pepys coughed again. She got up and held his head until he'd finished, then wiped his mouth with a cold cloth, and gave him a tiny sip of water.

She frowned at him. "Unfortunately, I think you'll live."

"Do you?" He blinked. The bad eye was beginning to blur again. "I wish I had your faith."

"Faith about what," Vandover said, as he entered the care unit. "Pepys, you're looking better."

"What's happening?"

The minister looked at Amber. There was an expression deep in those dark eyes that Pepys had never seen before and wasn't sure he liked. "Can't keep him down. K'rok has ordered a fallback to avoid a bloodbath. A good decision, I think—we don't need to give them any more martyrs at this point than they already have."

"What are you doing in the way of containment?"

Amber looked away. Pepys caught the expression of distance that had fallen across her features. If only he had not given over her destiny into Baadluster's hands. If only he had thought more about the decision. Concern made him cough again, and this time, no one moved to his aid. By the time he had caught his breath, the corridor had filled with noise as battle armored soldiers filed in.

Chapter 22

"They'll fight for me," Pepys said later, with confidence, his voice no longer a whisper, but thin and reedy for all that. The day had been long and the din from the armor in the hallways tumultuous. He felt weary unto death, but he clung to his wakeful state as if it were the only indicator that he still lived. All was quiet now.

Amber's suit hung in the corner of the care unit, near the life monitors. She eyed it as she stabbed a piece of protein from her packaged dinner. "They'll fight to survive. What's important, your highness, is that the two objectives coincide." She delicately picked the morsel from her fork and ate it.

Pepys stared at her. He debated about chiding her for the lack of respect in her tone of voice, but he knew Amber well . . . and knew that manners were like a suit of clothes to her, that she used them depending on whether or not she needed the disguise. He ended up sighing. She was right, of course. Wired to this crèche he was as helpless as a scraggly, thrown-away babe. He began to understand what Jack had seen in her, beyond her grace and beauty. She had an innate ability to filter the truth out, however fine, and retain its clarity. "I made a mistake with you," he said, to his utter surprise.

She shot him a look then, with such hatred in her eyes that he shrank back. It faded as quickly as he recognized it and Pepys wondered if he had really seen it at all. "Tell me you tampered with Jack and I'll unhook your crèche right now."

His shallow breathing rose and fell only with the help of that unit. He would get better, but for now . . . she threatened his very life. Pepys waved a hand, a reflection of his old imperious self, unaware that he did so. "On the contrary, I did all I could to help him."

"Then it was Vandover."

He nodded, a feeble movement that merely dropped his chin to his chest and left it there.

Amber's face twisted. "We're all spiders in that web." She polished off the last of her dinner, crumpled the packet as if it were an enemy, and tossed it away.

"But I left you to him," Pepys said softly, so softly that he was not even sure she'd heard him as she stood and crossed the room to her armor. It was coated with norcite, which gave it a gleam over its blue-black enameling. He thought it was a dark and deadly color for a beautiful woman. Did she murmur something back, or was it an unconscious echo of his own mind? *I made a mistake with you as well.*

His eyes felt terribly heavy. She had already fed him and now his thoughts spun away as quickly as a cloud across the merciless Malthen sky. "I think . . . I'll sleep now," he said.

"Good." Amber did not turn. The last thing he saw was a bleary image of her stretching out her hand and stroking the empty sleeve of the war suit.

He awoke to thunder. The corridors were filled with suits, running, and Amber came to his side, angling the crèche bed up so he could see better. Strain showed on her face.

"What is it?"

"They've fallen back. I'm not sure—"

One of the colossal armored bodies entered the care unit. Jack took off his helmet and hung it from his belt clip.

"Jack—" Amber blurted, then bit her lip as he gave her no notice.

He approached the emperor, had eyes for him alone. "We've been holding a defensive position." Sweat slicked back his sandy hair. Pain faded the blue of his eyes. "We can't hold it any longer, and I'll tell you, sir, that none of us wants to stage a full-scale war against what we're facing out there. And there's a Thrakian mother ship overhead, threatening to come in as well. *They* won't think twice about fighting."

Pepys wet his lips. "Vandover," he croaked, then took a sip of water from a glass Amber held for him. "Where is Vandover?"

"Monitoring Ash-farel activity. Something is happening out there. I've got to get to Colin. We can't wait any longer."

Pepys licked his lips again. "Speaker," he got out. "Hook me up to a speaker."

Jack watched the curtain of night. Flames of light spouted upward, orange-red against the blackness, then sputtered out. He could hear the percussion of explosions and the high-pitched singing of laser fire. His helmet bumped the hip of the suit. Against the relative silence of muted battle came the weakened voice of the emperor.

"This is Emperor Pepys. People of the Triad Throne, you work to your own undoing. Lay down your arms. Give our mission safe passage to search for St. Colin. I call on you to come to the bargaining table, not the battlefield."

The message repeated endlessly for nearly half an hour. Jack replaced his helmet and focused his cameras and sensors, searching for a response to the message being broadcast. None came. He had not expected any. He opened his com line.

"K'rok. They're calling our bluff. Give the signal. Rawlins, prepare to move out. Lassaday—watch your nuts." He fell back, anticipating renewed attack. Inside the suit, sweat dripped off his brow. He felt suffocated. His thoughts and memories tangled again. Where was he? *When* was he? He was a *Knight*, for god's sake, fighting the "Pure" war. He held onto that tenet as if it were a lifeline and strode into the night.

K'rok swelled out of his suit neckline as he removed his helmet. "I am being sorry, Minister," he said to Vandover. "We have done all we could, without a massacre."

Vandover paced the length of Pepys' care unit, his long black robes alive with the movement like a pair of immense wings at his back. He gave the Milot an ugly stare. "You don't win battles by retreating."

"No, sir." The Milot met his look, baring yellow-ivory canines of immense length. "But there will be another fight."

"Where's Jack?" Amber asked quietly in the tense silence that followed K'rok's statement.

"He be coming in last. There was a suit down, and the Dead Man circuit was triggered. The armor is lost, but our man might be injured. Jack be looking for our lost man."

"What about the Thrakian contingent of the guard?"

K'rok gave an eloquent shrug which the Flexalinks copied, a wave of movement down the length of the battle armor. Whatever he might have said was lost in the commotion at the corridor's end as the doors were opened up to the outside and Jack came in, bearing an injured man in his arms.

"Let's get this man in a crèche."

Fire and smoke framed him in the doorway. There was a moment of hesitation, then Rawlins leapt to his aid, his own suit gored and charred. Jack himself turned to secure the doors he'd come through. As they clanged shut, he removed his helmet and took deep gulps of air. Lassaday handed him a cold glass of beer. Jack took it and then grinned.

"Short rations, eh?"

The sergeant gave a bellowing laugh in response before trailing his men to the care unit where they swiftly installed the wounded Knight. Jack watched them go before sucking down a deep draught. Vandover met him in the corridor outside Pepys' room.

"What now?"

"We don't shield, at least, not yet. Can't afford

the power drain. This building can take an assault or two without damage." Jack paused for another drink. He rested the cooling glass against his forehead. "We need time." He saluted K'rok with his drink. "Commander."

"Commander," returned the Milot. He shouldered past Jack and for a moment the corridor was filled floor to ceiling with battle armor. The Milot growled, "I could use one of those."

Jack let him by. He smiled at Amber and Pepys and said, "It's going to be a long night."

Vandover scowled heavily. "What do you think you're doing?"

"Well, Baadluster, we're fighting the battle and right now, we're taking a break while the other side regroups and does some thinking. You see, up until now, we've only been deflecting them. We've done some heavy damage without being on the offensive. Even though we're dealing with fanatics here, some cooler heads are going to realize the kind of damage we can do if we take the offensive. Someone's going to hesitate." Jack paused for another drink. He lifted the empty glass in salute to Vandover. "You've got to remember that none of these people here have ever really seen us in combat. A demonstration or two in the stadium, but that's it. Now they have. Now they know just what to be scared of." He stifled a mild burp. "And now, if you'll excuse me, I'm going to get some sleep." He crossed the care unit and sat down, the Flexalink suit folding gracefully to lower him to the hard floor. He leaned his head back against the wall and closed his eyes.

Amber knew Vandover shot an angry glare at her, but she refused to meet his expression. She took up her post, curling up on a countertop, bracing her shoulders where the cabinet met the wall.

Pepys was either chuckling to himself or snoring lightly as Vandover made a disgusted noise and left the care unit.

The clangor came just before dawn. Jack got to his feet quickly, heading toward the secured doors. Rawlins, Lassaday, and K'rok joined him immediately. Pepys made a mewling noise as Amber sat him up a little. He seemed disoriented, then grasped her sleeve as she said, "Watch Jack."

"Open the doors," he ordered.

"Commander, scanners show they're—"

"I know what they are," Jack snapped, interrupting. "Get those doors open."

Lassaday pointed and two privates hurried to unshield and unbar the portal. It came open, the stink of smoke and ash flooding in.

Jack stepped forward. "General Guthul. How fortunate you've dropped in. We place ourselves at your mercy."

Amber gasped in disbelief as Storm knelt at the feet of the Thrakian warrior.

"I wish," Pepys said peevishly, "that someone had told me about all this."

Wearing her own armor and shouldering her pack, Amber said, "You're out of the loop, emperor. And so, apparently, am I." She pointed at the Thraks rolling the crèche out into the loading dock. "Watch it, bugface." She looked around the grounds, where landing ships had fused the landscape into a burnt, glassy surface. "Your gardeners are going to be real pissed."

Pepys laughed in spite of himself. The rose obsidite walls of the palace stood with scarcely a scar, but the grounds surrounding it looked as if they'd been through a firestorm. The carnage had marked them deeply. He could only thank K'rok's and Jack's intuition that the Walkers would hesitate before a full-scale Thrakian attack. Letting the allies come in had begun a cease-fire. The bad news was that Guthul was taking them in hand. Queen Tricatada wanted to talk to Pepys very badly. He dared show no weakness before the Thrakian queen.

Amber patted Pepys on the shoulder as if knowing his hesitant thoughts. Vandover led the caravan, his hands filled with the valises he carried, his shoulders bowed under the weight. Jack and the small handful of Knights going with them took up the rear. "It's going to be a rough trip," she commented, looking at the shuttle docked in a makeshift berth as they approached it.

"I'll make it," Pepys said grimly.

"You don't have much choice," Amber returned. She looked at the Thraks flanking them. They were as much prisoners as allies. She twisted about to glance at Jack. He'd been strangely quiet since his capitulation to Guthul, his longtime nemesis. She could not fathom what was going on behind his pale, careful expression.

Jack watched the loading caravan approach the shuttle. His thoughts slipped and tumbled over one another. He was walking into the enemy's jaws and none of them would make it out again if he couldn't keep himself together. He fought to hold on, to stay in control just one moment longer. Fatigue and stress leeched his strength when he needed it most. He would have stumbled, but the suit held him up, kept him moving. He looked at K'rok and for a frightening instant, Milos and Malthen overlapped one another, time over time.

The Milot brushed against him lightly, the jarring clearing his mind again, and he ducked his head as they reached the loading bay. The Thraks ensconced them all in hammocklike seats, the bay closed, and the ship began to thrum as it powered up.

Jack closed his eyes against the hammering thrust of the takeoff. He could hear Pepys' moaning over the roar of the engines. The little man might not survive the gs of the takeoff although the aneurysm was supposed to have been lasered off and cauterized, its damage already having been done. Would he care if Pepys died? He had time for no further wondering as the shuttle left its berth and the body-crushing punishment of leaving Malthen's gravity began. His memories could take no more.

He awoke to find Thraks unwrapping his armor from takeoff netting. They chittered in derision at his weakness. Jack put his boots on the floor and straightened, standing head and shoulders taller than their own giant forms. He looked about and saw the other humans and knew his own actions were hostage to theirs. He had been defeated and why he was not dead, he did not know. Flanked by Thraks, he was marched out of the shuttle and into the belly of a much larger vessel, probably a mother ship.

As they crossed the hangar, he saw the dais and the honor guard flanking the brilliant iridescent blue body of a queen Thraks. She levered herself upward, her face plates settling into a mask of exotic beauty as she looked at him.

"Welcome, my valorous warrior," she said to Guthul, speaking in the humans' language for the prisoners' sakes, then repeating it in her chirps and trills. The warrior Thraks made a deep obeisance to her.

The gorge rose in Jack's throat. He could bring the queen down from where he stood, but that meant that all of the prisoners' lives would be forfeit. He weighed the option as the queen turned to him.

"I bring you Commander Jack Storm," Guthul said formally. "Of whom you have heard so much sung about."

Sung? Caught off guard, he watched as a hangar door opened to her right. She indicated it.

"I have a surprise for you, Jack Storm, befitting your status as a warrior."

As the portal opened, his breath caught in his chest. Pearly armor faced him, helmet set beside its boots, scarred from battle and gallant—his armor, lost to the ages. Now he knew what his captors intended for him—he would be fed to his own armor, and left to be consumed by the parasite infesting it. *They* knew, the Thraks did, of the horrors of the Sand Wars on Milos.

Jack lunged at the armor, intent upon destroying it, upon ripping out the bestial life-form inhabiting it.

Amber screamed. "Jack! Don't! It's Bogie!"

Chapter 23

Under the weight of Jack's attack, the battle armor dropped to its knees, swaying. Amber lunged at him and hung on to his sleeve, crying, "Jack, don't do this."

He shook her off unthinkingly. Guthul moved to place himself between his queen and Jack, but Tricatada stopped him.

"It is his to deal with," she said, intrigued.

Jack reached into the neck of the armor where a chamoislike thing pulsed, woven within and without the gadgetry of the war suit. It was alive and yet not—unformed, embryonic—and it controlled the armor. Its empty sleeves clawed beseechingly upon his own armor.

Amber got to her feet. "No," she said. "I won't let you. *Don't make me do this.*"

His mind felt as though a whirlwind was blasting through it, tossing leaves of thought and memory to and fro, forward and backward, spinning around. Milos and Malthen, Dorman's Stand and *sand* . . . he awoke to find himself with his gauntlet down Bogie's gullet, with Amber's voice ringing in his ears.

He turned to look at her. She stood defiantly, chin out, engulfed by her own war suit, only her face and tangled mane of hair visible. Bright color illuminated her fine cheekbones and he knew he had not imagined what he remembered her saying. *Don't make me hurt you.* He could feel the edge of her mind now, like a blade against his neck. With great restraint, he kept himself from turning and looking at Pepys.

He knew now what she had done to protect herself and him when she thought she'd lost him. He knew now what had struck the emperor down. She had somehow gone and retrieved that dark part of herself they had worked so hard to purge— reimprinted herself, perhaps, just as he had done—and now she stood ready to protect Bogie as well.

He withdrew his hand, swallowing down a tightness in his aching throat. The near empty armor stopped clawing at him and slumped to its side. Jack kept himself from responding to Bogie's weakness. He must have gone berserk when he'd seen it. Rawlins stood guard over Pepys, his visor shielding his youthful expression. Jack wondered what he must think of his erratic commander.

"I am curious," Tricatada trilled, "as to what animates the armor."

I'll bet you are, Jack thought. "Robotics," he said.

"Curious," Guthul said, edging his body between them. "I thought robot arms were banned by your races."

"They are," Vandover Baadluster interjected smoothly. "This was an experimental model to retest them. As you can see, it is a failure."

Jack hooked his old helmet onto his belt and hefted the white armor in his arms. "It will be destroyed as soon as we can retrieve the data."

The Thraks turned her attention to him again. "Data?"

"This armor was with St. Colin when he disappeared. It's a good assumption that our in-suit cameras will have some recording of the incident."

"Ahhh." She waved a signal to Guthul. "I am pleased that we have salvaged it for you, then. Your quarters have been made ready. Then we shall talk."

Amber entered his quarters on his heels and knocked his gauntlets away as he set the collapsed armor down in a corner. She'd shed her suit and was still breathless with the effort as she knelt down by Bogie.

"What are you doing?"

She didn't look up at him but her voice was filled with scorn. "I'm powering your armor." With deft hands and a few small probes and tools she had secreted about a jumpsuit he could have sworn was skintight, she rigged a plug-in for the armor. When she was done, she swiveled on her heels. "You wouldn't want to lose all your precious *data.*"

Boss. Bogie's voice, its basso profundo tone a mere shadow of itself. *You have found me. And Amber is angry.*

Amber is indeed angry, but don't let her know we've talked.

The war suit shifted. Amber made a pleased sound and stroked it as if the Flexalinks could feel her touch. With Bogie hooked up inside it, it could.

I am a signpost, the being told him. *Colin said for me to point the way.*

Jack felt a thrill go through him. "We'll check it out later," he said aloud. "The systems look pretty drained."

Amber got to her feet then. "Don't let anybody else at this suit. It knows too much."

He met her level gaze. "Why did you threaten me?"

"I had no other way to stop you from harming . . . Bogie."

"It's a parasitic infestation."

Amber tossed her head. "It's *alive*, Jack and at least it knows who it is!"

He blocked her from leaving the tiny cabin cubicle. "Maybe you should tell me who I am."

Her hands worked. "You're a back-assed farm boy who just fell off the shuttle and wouldn't amount to slag if it hadn't been—hadn't been for me."

He couldn't take the pain in her voice and eyes any longer. He made a decision he hoped he wouldn't regret and answered, "I thought I was your White Knight."

Her mouth made a tiny "o." Then she kicked the door shut behind her and ran at Jack. He opened his arms to take her in, saying, "Quietly, quietly, we're not out of harm's way yet."

But instead of hugging him, she pommeled the chest of the armor until her hands were red with pain and he finally got hold of her.

"Son of a bitch," she cried and put her face to the Flexalinks. He could feel her shoulders heave with emotion. "What you've put me through."

"I know," he said softly, leaning down and putting his mouth to her ear. Mixed with the soft perfume that was uniquely hers, he could smell the plastic and metallic flavor of the armor she'd been wearing. "They tampered with my imprinting. For days I had no current memory. Now it slips and slides. Pepys has all but told me it was Vandover and to watch my back."

She snuffled. "Pepys is no angel either."

"I know. Amber . . . I know what you've done."

She pulled back. She looked up at him. She shook her head slowly. "No, I don't think so."

"I know about Pepys."

Something shadowed her golden-brown eyes. Then she shook her head again. "I couldn't help it. Are you going to turn me in?"

"No. Whether they've declared it or not, this is war, and," he smiled, "I need you on my side."

"Always."

"It's going to be painful. Until we're in the clear, until I've got a vessel and what I need to go after Colin, I have to keep you at arm's length."

She took a deep breath and answered, "I think I can make it that far."

He released her then. She gained the door and stopped. "What about Bogie? What happened to you just now?"

"I thought I was back on Milos . . . the evacuation . . . I'm not always here."

"And when you're not here . . . you're there?"

"Yes." He did not need to explain further. His torment reflected in her eyes.

"Still fighting the Sand Wars."

"Always."

She left him then, the tiny cabin growing darker as if she alone had kept it illuminated. Jack shook himself as he realized it was only Bogie, draining power. He went to the suit. "Now show me," he said, "what you know of Colin." Whatever he thought had happened, he was not prepared for what did happen—for the scream of fear and anguish Bogie had recorded.

Chapter 24

"There is a fine line between guests and prisoners, your majesty," Vandover said smoothly. "The slightest interruption in the power supply of my emperor's medical care unit can place him at risk. Intelligence tells me that our troops have resecured the palace grounds and the city-state known familiarly as Upper Malthen. I urge you to return us there, before we stage any further talks." Baadluster held the center of attention in the hangar as they gathered for a conference. The queen's dais had been moved into the loading dock as had Pepys' crèche. Amber hung behind Jack and watched them all intently, particularly K'rok, who now flanked his queen and general.

The queen hummed as the Minister of War spoke, her faceted eyes watching them all in turn with a placid, even benevolent expression on her mask. "Who is in charge if Pepys is weak?"

"I am his co-counsel, majesty, and let me assure you that Pepys is not weak, merely incapacitated for the moment. He speaks for himself and I do his will. As for the Triad Throne—"

"Shut up, Vandover," Pepys said, face white.

"The Triad Throne is secure in all respects—"

"*Shut up*, Vandover," the emperor repeated, his

187

crèche fairly shaking with agitation. Rawlins moved toward it protectively, but Pepys waved him off.

Tricatada let out a trill which Jack interpreted as laughter. The Thrakian ruler bent down. "Let us discuss this incapacitation."

"A stroke, your highness, an attack upon the brain." Vandover smiled thinly.

Pepys glared at Vandover, but said nothing.

"Pepys, do you expect to return to your throne?"

"Yes," he answered loudly, a spark of his old self apparent in his words. "I warn you, Tricatada, that any effort by you to go beyond those measures allowed by our convention of alliance will be construed by myself as an act of war." His eyes flashed.

Amber murmured to Jack, "He doesn't sound afraid that she might pull his plug."

"He can't," Jack answered back carefully. "The Thraks don't believe in wounded or infirm. They take no prisoners."

"Unless they're stocking the larder." She shifted her weight. "What's K'rok up to?"

"I'm not sure." Jack watched the Milot. He got the impression the commander was aiding with the finer nuances of translation, but he had no real confirmation of that. Did Guthul or Tricatada know how close K'rok had come to throwing away his allegiance altogether? Had the Walker forces been smaller or less adamant, K'rok would not be standing with them now. He listened to Tricatada giving Pepys assurances of their actions. It was impossible to tell if the Thraks had a patronizing tone.

When Tricatada finished her speech, she turned

to Jack. "What news do you have of your missing man?"

Her directness took him aback. "I report to my superiors, majesty, and the information you ask me to divulge is privileged. The power drain on my armor was severe and the recordings damaged, but I do know Colin was in search of the Ash-farel, hoping to make peaceful contact. How he predicted that they would come to Claron, I don't know. But he was right and he left enough data for me to follow."

"Follow the Ash-farel," the queen repeated. "With what purpose? He had been named envoy by you, Pepys? What could he have had in mind?"

Jack's gaze flicked to the emperor.

"Come now, Storm," Guthul said. "Your emperor and minister ask us for a vessel and outfitting for your mission. There must be a price paid for everything." He rattled his chitin in emphasis, like an irritated beetle. "And the armor is a gift from my queen."

Jack frowned at him. "I'd like to ask just how you acquired it, if we're trading information."

"Jack," Vandover soothed, as Guthul drew himself upward.

The Thrakian general sputtered as his queen rearranged her mask. "This is a fitting question," she answered. "We were investigating Ash-farel intrusion in the quadrant which contains the rehabilitating planet Claron. This intrusion was most unique. It appeared to be a reconnoitering flight . . . something our ancient enemy rarely does. We found a rescue pod, a tiny vessel, from a larger Walker cruiser. It was empty except for the armor. It tried to defend the vessel, but its resources were too drained. Why, Minister Baadluster, would a Walker be this far out? We have had several encounters with those of the Walker persuasion. We seem to have similar interests in norcite deposits."

"I'm afraid the norcite veins are coincidental to the archaeological sites which are also near. The Walkers, while in need of funding, are not interested in mining norcite. It has a very limited market. They will mine gold and platinum deposits if located, but they are most interested in the archaeological finds." Baadluster put his hands behind his back and took a stance. Oddly, it mirrored Guthul's position near his queen.

Tricatada leaned close to K'rok and a slender but muscular, lean-bodied drone all but hidden by the Milot's bulk. She trilled and chirped with the two of them for a few moments. Hearing K'rok imitate Thrakian speech was a different experience, Jack decided. After a moment, the queen looked up. Her blue carapaces shimmered as she gestured.

"If the Walkers have no use for norcite as we do, yet we find them disputing our mining claims so often, who is to say they do not seek to negotiate those claims with our enemy? And if this is so, why should we aid those who might be the friends of our enemy?"

"One might ask us the same of you," Jack said tightly.

Guthul swung on him. "You are a warrior," he spat out in Thrakian agitation. "You presume to answer for your emperor? You presume to have your speech inflicted upon my queen? I will not tolerate your insults. I have heard far too much from you already."

Vandover apologized, but General Guthul was alive with quivering movement. Jack's lips drew into a fine line as he recognized the Thrakian battle rage. He gave a hand signal to Rawlins. The shock-haired officer took it in and answered with a grave nod. He was prepared to die protecting Pepys' crèche.

Jack looked to Pepys. "A Thraks' concept of a ruler is different from ours, your highness. As the only fertile egg-layer, a Thrakian queen is solely responsible for the continuation of their race. She approaches godhood in status. Your responsibility, Pepys, is far exceeded by hers. However, failure in any ruler is not tolerated by those ruled," he ended deliberately, shifting the Thraks' attention from his emperor to himself.

There was a snap in the air as the queen's wings thrashed out, a canopy spanning those two or three near her as well as herself. Amber made a sound of awe at Jack's back.

"I didn't know she had those."

The awesome spectacle of the queen's wingspan took him by surprise as well. "I didn't either," he answered, as he took a step backward, taking Amber with him. It was his fault the queen had taken umbrage over a remark he had meant for Pepys. He had forgotten for a moment her inability to lay another queen. At the opening snap, Guthul had gone prone where he knelt still, head down, at his monarch's feet.

Vandover looked toward Jack, his blotchy face ashen. "Someone," he said in an undertone, "must pay for this."

Jack nodded. "It was my insult. Let Guthul take it out of my hide."

K'rok moved forward as Guthul raised upward, his mask frozen in hideous Thrakian fury. Amber held onto Jack's arm. "Don't."

"I have to. They'll only outfit us if they think we're strong enough to take what we want anyway. How do you think K'rok's stayed in her graces this long? She knows he's never really capitulated to her. The Thraks don't respect the weak."

"You can't fight him unarmored," Pepys husked from his crèche. His spark had gone and he seemed shrunken, weary.

Rawlins seconded him. "It's suicide, Commander."

K'rok interrupted. "My queen has taken offense from your remark, friend Jack. My commander is bringing challenge to you."

"And I accept, K'rok."

The hairy Milot bent closer. "You have hit home. She fears that you know her innermost shame. Guthul will not rest until you're dead, but I don't think she will be allowing that."

"Tell her I fight for Pepys' honor as well as my own. She thinks him too weak to rule ... she's toying with all of us now."

The Milot inclined his shaggy head. "You be knowing her well, Jack." He stepped back and spoke rapidly to the Thraks.

Guthul snarled back. K'rok gestured and humped his shoulders. Amber's hands tightened on Jack's arm. "What's happening? Are we going to get out of here?"

"We're as good as prisoners if the queen doesn't

respect our ability to assert ourselves. Vandover can spread as many honeyed words as he wants—it won't get us a ship to go after Colin, or get Pepys back to Malthen."

Vandover had moved to the other side of Pepys' medical crèche, standing over him like a storm cloud. "They wouldn't dare harm us."

Jack let out a humorless laugh. It drew Guthul's attention and the two stared at each other across the hangar floor. "You see," Jack said quietly. "He wonders what we're laughing about. He wonders how we can be so brazen as to laugh now, in the midst of crisis. The only way to get respect out of a Thraks is to beat it out of him."

Guthul dropped his hard stare and chattered rapidly at K'rok. The Milot officer made a motion with his pawlike hands. The Thraks gestured abruptly.

K'rok turned around. "The challenge is agreed to. Guthul has asked for personal combat."

Amber thrust herself forward, her hair flying with her movement. "Not under those terms. Jack is bare-handed." Jack pulled her back, but the Milot stared at her for a few instants.

K'rok showed his teeth. "A moment, little missy." He turned back and argued briefly with the Thraks. Then he came around again. "Jack, as befits a Knight, in armor. Guthul will be wearing Thrakian bracers."

Jack thought rapidly. His new armor was still being powered. The only armor he had that was fit to wear was his old armor. He shuddered as his memories warred with one another, and the Sand Wars won. He had no desire to wear an infested battle suit. K'rok drew close. His rumbling voice lowered. "You must be wearing your old suit, Jack. It is the only way. I know the secret of norcite. The Thraks eat it powdered to strengthen their body armor. Your old suit has been enameled with it. Guthul will not be seeing you so easily . . . he will be thinking it another Thraks."

The Milot looked at him intently. Jack nodded, momentarily confused. Who was he? He got a grip on himself as he considered the importance of what the Milot had told him, and whether K'rok could be trusted. Norcite . . . eaten by the Thraks? He watched K'rok rejoin the queen, Guthul, and her drone. The difference between the drone and the warrior Thraks was astounding—but the Thraks bred for that difference. And had begun to ingest norcite to augment it. Eaten a tremendous amount of it, if their avid search for new norcite deposits was any indication.

How had the Milot known? Jack only knew of one man beyond the Thrakian League who might have known that secret—and Mierdan was safely hidden among the Green Shirts' ranks. The little xenobiologist had spent more than twenty years among the Thraks and since Jack had brought him home, Tricatada had searched tirelessly for him. It was Mierdan who had told Jack why the Thraks swarmed so militantly, because of their sterility, in a desperate attempt to prolong their existence.

He gently shook Amber off and stepped forward. Tricatada still extended her wingspan, colors shimmering in the hangar's lighting. "I welcome the opportunity to prove my bravery," he said, watching her. He was careful not to let his interior battle show . . . old Jack and young Jack, as he'd grown to think of himselves. Young

Jack was thrilled to fight Guthul but feared his own armor. Old Jack was dismayed to fight yet again but trusted Bogie. As both identities tried to possess him, he eyed the Thrakian queen. Her body was full and pulsing—did she swell with eggs yet again?

Was Malthen destined to become the next *sand* world if they failed here and now to convince the Thraks of their ability to hold the Triad Throne? Pepys had taken a grave chance in allying with this enemy. The queen's throat leather swelled. "And if you win, Pepys' champion, we will abide by our alliance and will return Malthen to its rightful ruler, and you will be given our fastest ship to go after St. Colin. If you lose . . . we must talk long and hard about our futures."

"How are you doing?"

Sweat sprang up on his brow as he closed the inner seams and the chamois that was Bogie settled about his shoulders and down his bare back. "I'm fine."

Amber looked at him. "You don't look fine."

He fought the impulse to tear the armor from him as his mind warred against itself. "I'm losing it," he said.

She mopped the perspiration from his brow with the palm of her hand, and combed his hair away from his face with gentle fingers. "Try to hang on."

He nodded and busied himself clipping leads on his torso before putting his arms into his sleeves.

Boss, rumbled Bogie comfortingly. For a moment, their emotions entertwined, and he felt the jubilant warrior spirit that was the other. What was Bogie, anyway, if not a Milot berserker? *I am a signpost* the other answered him.

The road to Colin and truth.

"I have to make this a good fight," Jack said. "We can't afford to have Bogie damaged."

Amber paused in her work on his left gauntlet. She smiled gently. "Jack, he'll fry you."

"Only if he gets the chance. Why do you think K'rok maneuvered me into armor? He wants to bring the general down as Tricatada's right hand ... why, I don't know, but he's always followed his own game plan. Give me the helmet." He shoved his arms into his sleeves, felt the electric tingle at his wrists telling him he was powered up and armed, as Amber gave him his helmet. He screwed it in place.

The outside world was not muffled away, but keener and sharper than ever before. Bogie's hard-wired senses joined into those of the armor made it like a second skin. He was aware of every curve and nuance of Amber's body as she leaned forward into the Flexalinks, checking the helmet's fit. He felt himself sifting emotions and thoughts.

"Let me go," he said. "I'm as ready as I'll ever be."

"All right." She pushed a tangle of tawny hair back. "Whatever happens, I'll be backing you up."

Her expression was serious and Jack knew she meant what she said. He started to nod, stopped because that was one of the few movements the suit could not imitate, and saluted her instead.

"I shall kill him," Guthul promised his queen.

"I would be pleased," Tricatada murmured. "I want Malthen for our own, and this alliance has grown as cumbersome as an old egg casing." She stroked her warrior's brow. "Do as little damage to the armor as you can, now that we know its worth. Handled properly, it will lead us to the nest of our ancient enemy and we can at last strike at their vulnerable undersides."

Guthul froze under her touch, his desires raging. Her body glistened with the egg sacs swelling inside of her—*his* get, *his* seed—and without a doubt, one of them might well prove to be the savior of their race. He would not fail her. She dropped her arm/leg as if guessing the fever of his thoughts.

"I will be watching," she sang to him.

The loading hangar had been cleared. The audience watched from above, from mechanics' booths. Pepys labored in his crèche and Amber put a hand on his shoulder. He was cool to her touch. She immediately ordered a covering, and prepared to watch over the emperor. She had done this, and if she could give her own life to undo it, she would. He had never shown any fear or suspicion of her and guilt bit into her deeply. He patted her hand back.

"You need to be home," she said. For this man, this enemy who had so confounded her and Jack's lives, she found pity and understanding when she would rather have hated him. If this had been Vandover instead of Pepys—she would have struck him dead, but instead she found herself grasping the creed that motivated the emperor.

"Jack knows more about the Thraks than just about any man alive," Pepys said. He did not notice the sharp look Vandover gave him suddenly.

The emperor let go of Amber's hand. "Here they come."

The metal hangar clanged and thrummed as the stock portals opened and let the two combatants into it.

Even to onlookers from above, they had not lost their grace or immense stature as they approached one another in a *pas de deux de guerre*. Amber tightened her grip on Pepys' shoulder. She did not know if she could strike quickly enough to save Jack's life, if it came to that, or even if she could strike at all, the Thraks were so alien. Her glance slid away from Jack and Guthul as they sized one another up, thinking that if she could strike, it would be at Vandover.

As if sensing her thoughts, the Minister of War looked up. His brown hair had an unhealthy luster in the booth's dim light. His thick lips curled. "Good luck to your commander, milady," he said.

Amber shivered. She looked back to the battle. Rawlins shifted beside her, equally intent on what was happening below.

Jack let Guthul strike first, determining the method of combat they would be using. The Thraks wore wrist lasers, signaling his intent to do some serious damage if Jack's shields ever weakened. Jack couldn't remember ever having engaged in hand to hand combat with a Thraks, but he knew of those who had—literally torn from their armor. That was why suits came with a Dead Man circuit, to destroy the armor rather than let it fall into enemy hands. A Thraks could be incredibly strong, though Jack believed that battle rage enhanced the power.

Bogie still lacked full power. The suit could not keep his body heat down properly. Sweat poured off his face, blurred his eyesight and one of the leads clipped to his torso slipped off with a snap. Bogie pulsed across his shoulder blades. *Go for the throat leather, boss.*

"I just want to bring him down." Jack felt the armor rock back on its heels as the Thraks reared and kicked out. The shock drilled him to the roots of his teeth.

I think he wants us in pieces, boss Bogie rumbled back. Jack got in motion, using all the strength and agility of his war suit, hitting the power vault.

Guthul matched him, malice glittering redly in his dark, faceted eyes. Then Jack spun away and for a split second, hesitation was masked on the Thraks' face. He's lost me, Jack thought, and then the Thraks responded as Jack landed and pivoted, but not fast enough to evade the Knight as Jack threw him across the hangar floor. Sparks flew as the wrist lasers dragged across the metal plating under Guthul.

K'rok had been right. There was something about the battle armor that Guthul could not quite see—but even as Jack realized it, Guthul fired and the wash of the energy threw Jack off his knee and rolling across the hangar floor. He could feel the heat through his second skin.

The armor could take so much fire—was made for it—but with his evaporation and temperature regulation systems down—enough fire would be the death of Jack. He'd cook inside the suit. He did a backward flip out of harm's way of a second blast, and leapt to close instead, where armed fire would hurt Guthul as much as himself.

As they closed, the hangar floor vibrated under them. Guthul slammed Jack in the chestplate. The blow reverberated into Jack's own chest. As he gasped for air, he kicked back and around, seeking to dislodge the Thraks. Guthul went down. He rolled quickly and came up. From the angle of the general's head, Jack knew the Thraks was looking for him.

But he could not move for a second, doing everything he could to just *breathe*, the wind knocked out of him. His lungs felt as though a giant fist squeezed them shut.

The Thraks came up. His sight scrolled past Jack. Jack blinked the sweat out of his eyes and gulped a swallow of air as his diaphragm loosened. *Son of a bitch*, K'rok had been more than right. Guthul could only spot him as long as he stayed in motion.

The Lasertown miners' gift of having had Bogie coated in norcite years ago had probably saved Jack's life several times over, since. With irony, Jack told Bogie that. The problem now was to defeat Guthul without destroying him and incurring the further wrath of the queen. And to defeat him, Jack would have to move, drawing the Thraks' attention.

"What's he doing?" Baadluster's face twisted.

"I don't know. Circuitry damage maybe—he took quite a hit."

Pepys sucked in a rasping breath. "He'll be all right."

"I know," Amber whispered. "I know."

"We're running out of time," Vandover protested. "He's got to move and move now."

As if in answer to his objection, the battle armor twisted and kicked high, just under Guthul's Kabuki mask of rage. The Thraks fell back, arms flailing in pain. Jack laid down a line of fire that scored the hangar plates, sending the Thraks leaping into his embrace. The two soldiers closed a last time and when Amber opened her eyes, the Thraks lay still on the floor, Jack's booted foot firmly on his throat leather, the only vulnerable spot on a Thrakian soldier's body.

They had won.

Chapter 25

The shuttle to Malthen lay in the bay of the mother ship, its ramps down and berth ready for disembarkation. Pepys rested in his crèche, waiting to be loaded, his breathing a little easier than it had been in days, but his color still pallid. K'rok shadowed him as the emperor reached out and took Jack's hand.

"Against all charges of desertion and treason, I hereby find you guiltless and absolved. Baadluster and Commander K'rok, witness me."

There was a hearty glint in the Milot's eyes as he growled, "I witness," his hale voice drowning out Vandover's quiet response.

Jack found a tremble in his hand as he removed it from the emperor's. "Why now?" he asked. "My job isn't done yet."

"You've earned it. If anything should happen to me or to you, this shadow will be lifted. You've protected me from everything but myself. I could not ask you to do more. This needed to be done now."

He eyed his emperor. "I'll be back," he said. "You promised me a throne." He stepped back as the Thraks approached.

Vandover turned his back on the aliens, his face

as dark and clouded as the robes he wore. "Pepys, I ask you to reconsider my returning with you. I prepared to go with Commander Storm and this change of plans is most distressing."

"I need you with me," Pepys answered simply.

"My value with St. Colin—"

"Your value is with me."

Baadluster shut his mouth. Then, shuttering away the abrupt look of hatred in his dark, flat eyes, he bowed his head and stepped out of the way so that the Thrakian guard could wheel the medical crèche up the ramp. As soon as Pepys was out of his sight, he wheeled on Amber and took her by the elbow. He bent his lips to her ear before she could pull away in startlement.

"Do not think yourself free of me. My thoughts will find yours wherever you hide."

He let go so suddenly she rocked back on her heels, even as she swung her head about to protest his catching her up.

"What was that about?" Jack said.

She shook her head. "A threat to remember him by," she answered quietly, troubled. She watched Vandover mount the ramp in Pepys' wake, never looking back. As the shuttle ramp pulled close, she felt him tug at her thoughts, unclean and revolting mental touch followed by his mocking laughter. Unconsciously, she stepped closer to Jack for protection.

K'rok dropped his heavy hand on Jack's shoulder. "Now it is my time to say good-bye." With his other hand, he signaled the Thraks to hold up securing the shuttle ramp. It paused, half-shut. "I am being given orders by my queen to go with Pepys."

"I thought you were going with us." An unexpected sadness washed through Jack.

"So I was also thinking. But Tricatada has asked me to go to make sure our alliance is strong." He scratched his thick jowl. "We each be facing our destinies now, Jack. Good luck to you."

Jack clasped the Milot's wrist. "And you, K'rok."

The brace of Thrakian guards began to chitter in agitation. K'rok answered them rapidly and strode across the dock's floor. He jumped to catch the ramp and as soon as his booted feet rang upon its surface, it began to close again.

Left with only Rawlins and Amber at his side, Jack watched the shuttle engines begin to burn. Amber pulled him through the air lock so the bay could be evacuated and then opened to space. Jack did not linger at the viewing portal. "Suit up," he told them. "I want them to see us leave in armor."

"Yessir," Rawlins said, and grinned.

Pepys mopped at the corner of his droopy eye. The crèche hindered him more than it aided him as the Thraks escorted him across the sere grounds of the palace. He snapped at Vandover, "I want the place staffed again, immediately. And get a medical team in—I want to be out of this thing as soon as possible. Get me a scooter instead. See to it."

Without replying, Vandover dropped back in the caravan so that Pepys could no longer see him as the crèche rolled past.

"I want the WP out here and this area kept secured. See if we can get them in armor if need be."

K'rok rumbled, "The suits are being dangerous to amateurs, emperor."

"Whatever it takes, then, Commander. I'm still emperor here and I think our citizens should know it."

The Milot gave a half-bow. "Your wish is my command."

"And Vandover—" Pepys attempted to twist around in his bed. "I want a listening post set up to keep track of what Storm is doing."

"Of course," Baadluster said neutrally. He gathered himself as if walking into a strong wind, chin down in thought. The battle-scarred ground crunched beneath his steps. Beyond the side yards, if he looked up, he could see the sentries set up and the sonic watch posts. In the far distance, if he listened, he could hear the faint "pop-pop" of artillery. But the war in Upper and Under-Malthen was nothing compared to the battle raging in his thoughts at the moment.

"We'll pick up a pilot on Claron. There'll be somebody there who's free-lancing; until then, we've got the auto. Rawlins here tells me he's been studying and can make manual adjustments if he has to."

The younger man looked at Jack, color high on his fair face. Amber laughed at Rawlins' reaction to the mild teasing. "Better you than a Thraks," she added.

Rawlins finally shrugged and strapped in. "They could have this baby rigged to blow, for all I know."

Jack sobered. "They don't. They're letting us go too easily. I think they have almost as much at stake in this venture as we do. They've been fighting the Ash-farel far longer—and all it's done is drive them father afield." He motioned Amber to a net. "Better settle in."

Rawlins maneuvered himself into a seat meant for a Thrakian pilot, his armor folding to meet the demands of his body. He looked the control board over. "They've ripped stuff out of here, sir. I think they're not too anxious for us to have one of their ships at our disposal." He pointed at the dash curving in front of him with open slots and blank areas where clips and leads dangled.

Jack scanned the board. "As long as we have what we need to make the trip."

"As near as I can tell."

"Then signal them to get the bay open. We've wasted enough time." Jack loomed over Rawlins a second or two longer, then backed toward his own webbing. Bogie brushed over his thoughts. Jack flinched away from the contact without thinking of his reaction. He could not bear to hear once again his friend's voice echoing in the scream of fear and anguish that Bogie had recorded. How long could a saint live in the hands of the enemy?

Long enough, he hoped, to be rescued.

Chapter 26

The physician shook her head as she watched the readout. "You will never be the man you were," she said to Pepys. The emperor squirmed in anger in the crèche.

"Never mind that," he said. "How soon can you get me out of this thing?"

The woman turned, and a slight smile warmed her cool features, drawing her almond eyes into a graceful curve. "That thing is what is keeping you breathing. Look here and here—these shaded areas are those affected by your stroke. That's permanent damage and, unfortunately, in an area where even repatterning will not be of very great benefit. This area here—" she traced it with a light pen—"we have bypassed the involuntary muscle stimulus center successfully. Yes, you'll be off the respirator soon—but your arm and leg will be permanently weakened. And you're extremely susceptible to another attack."

"Will I be competent or not?" Pepys' green eyes darkened as he glared at her.

"You'll be somewhat handicapped, but I suppose you'll be as competent as you wish to be . . . " Her soft voice trailed off.

"That is all I wanted to know. Vandover!" Pepys snapped.

The minister had been watching and listening to the examination with an abstracted expression of his own. He came to the bedside when the emperor summoned him. "Vandover, you're relived of the burden my illness placed on you."

"So soon? Perhaps you should wait until you are out of the crèche, at least. There are other susceptibilities. . . ." Baadluster's voice trailed off as the emperor struggled to sit up despite the shell of the respirator over his chest.

Pepys waved the physician out of the care unit. She left, whisper-quiet. As soon as the door shut behind her, he said, "Take care, Vandover. Take great care. Don't let your ambitions trip you up now. There is more than enough in all of this for both of us."

Baadluster held his breath until he had forced his emotions to calm. Then he answered, "You are a ruthless man."

Pepys smiled. "And it takes one to recognize that, does it not?"

Baadluster did not answer. The emperor plucked at the corner of his sheeting. "Do you still have your contacts among the Green Shirts?"

"Some."

"Good. I want you to spread the word that, when St. Colin is found, he will be held hostage against Walker good behavior."

The minister paused, then said, "That may not be necessary. I've gotten reports of renewed fighting between Thrakian forces and our outer continents. Even with the Green Shirts among them, how long can the Walkers hold out?"

Pepys lay back. Tricatada dared to invade anyway, under the guise of bringing the entire planet to order. Then he shrugged. "Well, then. As long as they are fighting each other, they cannot fight us."

"I shall keep that in mind." Vandover bowed gravely and left the emperor alone in his sick room, staring in thought. Then he called for Commander K'rok.

When the Milot commander turned up, he was slightly winded, his pelt ruffled as though he'd been in a rush. He smelled of laser fire and sweat. He came to a halt at Pepys' side, with a nod that was far less than subservient.

"Have you men I can trust?"

The Milot's eyes narrowed as if he'd been insulted. Pepys met his glare with an innocent expression. "I want a man to follow one of the WP."

"Ahh," the commander said. He frowned. "But the World Police are your own."

"No. Never mine. First Winton's and now, I fear, Vandover's."

"I be seeing," answered K'rok. "I have one or two we can trust."

"Good. Baadluster will be leaving the palace shortly, if he has not already. I want him followed. Recorded, if possible, but probably not—if he wanted to leave himself open to recording, he would communicate from here. No, he'll probably be shielded, but try anyway."

"I will have it done," K'rok rumbled.

Pepys nodded, closing his eyes, his flare of strength ebbing rapidly. His last waking thoughts carried the echo of the Milot's heavy footsteps leaving the care unit.

* * *

K'rok trusted the assignment to no one but himself. As torn and littered by warfare as the streets were, he wore armor and easily kept abreast of the vehicle Baadluster ordered up. The hover car wove painstakingly in and out of the warrens of the city while the Milot found the broken concrete canyons to his advantage, keeping to their shadows and barricades. When at last the automated vehicle came to a stop, Baadluster sat in it until another shadow joined him. K'rok keyed open his suit sensors to full capacity and watched his targeting grid in case other shadows thought of besieging him.

"Well done, Naylor," came Baadluster's reedy voice. "I thought to wait half the night for you."

"My bunker's not far from here. This area isn't secured, minister. This meeting isn't safe for either of us."

"Some risks are worth taking. Pepys is gathering in the reins of power again."

"Pepys?" Surprise in the other's voice. "I thought he'd had a severe stroke."

"It is not well for him, but he doesn't care if he walks or stands alone, as long as he can continue to govern alone. He will recover."

K'rok listened to an intake of breath, and then silence. There was then a sound as if something were being exchanged between hands.

"I've coded your instructions on this, but all depends on how well you've infiltrated the Walkers."

"You cannot separate one weave from the other."

Vandover's voice. "Good! You'll find this more

detailed. Bring them down, lay them open. I want them gutted."

Disbelief registered in the other's, this Naylor's, voice. "The Thraks will sweep through us."

"Precisely. Keep your men clear when it happens."

"And what'll happen then?"

"Then," answered Baadluster, "then thcy'll give me the Triad Throne."

K'rok's target grid showed him moving figures to his flank, and thcre was static over the receivers as the shadowy occupant left the taxi hastily. The Milot withdrew then, knowing he had heard all he could. He pondered his information as he returned to Upper Malthen, sifting through his memory, wondering what he would choose to tell Pepys and what he would not. It was clear to him that the emperor expected treachery. But did he expect collusion with the Thrakian League? In all probability not—or he would not have passed this task to K'rok.

Or perhaps he knew what K'rok had hidden in his own black heart.

Lengthening his stride, the Milot crossed the war zones of the city.

Pepys woke to thunder in the halls again— battle suits running the corridors. His heart took a skip and jump, and he peered through his one clear eye as the saggy one blurred. Dark armor loomed up beside him, and a heavy gauntlet fell upon his shoulder.

"Do not be worrying," K'rok said in his gravelly voice. Before he could say more, the emergency lights flickered on, and Baadluster swept in, illuminated by the orange glow.

"Arrest him," Baadluster ordered. His hand shook with fury as he targeted K'rok.

Armor flanked the corridor, but no one moved to do as Vandover ordered. The man looked from side to side as he realized his bidding was being ignored.

"I be thinking not," said K'rok. "These are Knights. I am a Knight." Pride echoed in his heavy voice.

"Explain this," Pepys got out. His voice croaked each word. He did not know if he felt reassured or threatened by K'rok's presence.

"I have purged your command of the Thraks," the Milot told him.

"You what?"

The bulky Flexalinked personage of Sergeant Lassaday bulled forward into the doorway. The sergeant cleared his throat. "There ain't a Thraks left among us. Sir." If he could have spat, he would have.

Pepys rubbed at his bleary eye carefully as if it might clear his perspective. "What did you do?"

"I be putting them on the shuttle and shipping them back. And I be allowing no further incoming landings."

Baadluster's mouth twisted. "Guthul will split a gut. Tricatada will lay waste to the entire planet if she thinks you've gone back on your alliance."

"Or you yours," Pepys said, watching K'rok intently as the Milot took his helmet off. The shaggy being grinned at him. He felt pleasure surge through him. He had guessed Vandover's game and here stood K'rok verifying it to him.

The Milot saluted. "I be commander of your Knights, emperor. We will die defending you."

Vandover gathered himself under his robes. Pepys now turned his gaze on his minister.

"Have you anything to say?"

"I," Baadluster ground out, "have nothing to say."

"That is very circumspect of you. I might almost suspect that you are waiting for the Thraks to break through. Would you wish that, minister?"

"They are our allies."

"Mmmm." Pepys then ran his hand through his red hair. The fine strands which had lain lankly upon his pillow since he'd been struck down, began to crackle and rise with electricity as though newly invigorated. "Well done, Commander," he said to K'rok. "Now pray you can hold this island free until Commander Storm returns."

"Aye," answered K'rok. "I be praying."

He remained at Pepys' side as Vandover left in a swirl of robes and anger, escorted down the corridor by Lassaday and the troops, as if knowing the emperor wished to talk to him privately. When they had been left alone, Pepys merely turned an inquiring stare on the Milot.

K'rok showed his teeth happily. "I be following him myself," he said. "He met with a Green Shirt by the name of Naylor."

Pepys sucked in a breath. "Verified?"

"Voice print ident."

"All right. Go on. I ordered him to do that."

"They met in under-Malthen, near the firing zones. He be ordering Naylor to abandon the Walker lines, leaving them open to Thrakian attack. He be thinking grateful Thraks would make him emperor."

"He's probably right, too. The Thraks abhor weakness. My . . . infirmity . . . would lead them to this, and Vandover would take advantage of it. Why didn't you come to me first?"

K'rok's shoulders rolled in an eloquent shrug. "You probably not be allowing me to do what I did."

Pepys gave a dry laugh. "Probably not," he agreed. "I owe you one."

"More than one, emperor. Shall I tell you the price now?"

They were alone in the shadowed hospital wing. Pepys suddenly felt cold, and shook it off. It would be better to know, he told himself. "All right."

"Who ruled Milos?"

"Your people did, under the aegis of the Triad Throne, of course—that's what we were doing there fighting, protecting you and the considerable Dominion investments." Pepys reflected that the loss of those investments were what had given him financial sway over the Dominion, which was in part why he and Winton and Baadluster had arranged the military defeat there, but he had no intention of telling K'rok that.

"And if the Thraks left Milos now?"

"Milos is *sand*, dammit, you thick-headed woolly. What use is it to anyone, even if the Thraks did pull out?"

"It's my home," K'rok rumbled.

The emperor heard the edge in his words. "Yes, I understand that. What are you asking of me?"

"I want to go back. I want to go back as governor and ruler of Milos."

Pepys shook his head. "Oh, please. I have no control over this—"

"The *sand* is failing. Did Storm not tell you?"

"No. No, he didn't. And how do you know?"

K'rok's eyes shone. "I never forget my home. Queen Tricatada is most distressed over Milos' failure. *Sand* comes from the first nest. It has never failed before. But now it has. She has thinned it too much, perhaps, overswarming. She does not know. I do not know, though I guess much. Milos will be abandoned. As long as you hold the Triad Throne, it is yours. Give it to me, Pepys. That is my price."

"As long as I hold the throne," Pepys repeated. "Done, Commander. Milos is yours if the Thraks should abandon it. More than that I cannot promise you."

The gauntlet squeezed tight on his shoulder. "That be fine. I will take care of the rest. Now we wait for Jack to come back."

Chapter 27

She awoke in fear and hunger, pain cramping in her stomach, her hands digging into her flesh as if she could knead it out. Agony lanced through her temples as her dreams leeched away into wakefulness amid the awful echo of Baadluster's laughter. She panted once or twice to clear her thoughts, but he'd been in them again and the smutty residue she could not cleanse.

A crowded room, an argument, a stern looking woman pointing at the man dressed richly in robes of crimson and gold, and the weapon of her mind lashing out. . . . She wouldn't do it again. Couldn't. She'd do whatever she had to, to keep Jack safe. *Milady.* A last, sickening jab from Baadluster and then he was gone for the moment. Her torment slowly ebbed away. The Thrakian hammock twisted about her as she got out, finally dumping her on the floor with a thud. Amber sat in the dim light. It was almost her turn on watch, anyway, and she knew that sleep was impossible now. She was getting to be like Jack, she thought ironically.

The hunger she could handle. They'd all eaten lightly for dinner, bypassing what the Thraks had stocked for meat. But there were legumes and dried fruits and even breads aplenty, so she picked out an assortment of baggies to take with her to the deck. There was no sense in shorting herself, the stores had been packed for a full crew and Jack figured they'd be pulling out of FTL and turning the corner for Claron within the next twenty-four hours. The three of them practically rattled around in the Thrakian cruiser.

Jack turned his head as she padded softly on deck and came to rest at his shoulder. He was getting used to her sleeplessness. The week or so they'd been aboard, she'd been early for every watch.

"What's up?"

"Nothing," he answered, turning his attention back to the screens. "We'll be going into decel and turning the corner in about nine hours. You'd better buckle up after you get off watch."

Amber made an "ummm" sound in her throat as she nodded. The lighting from the panels was subdued and had an odd coloration that she had no description for because it was in the visual spectrum of the Thraks. It cast an eerie glow over Jack's features, highlighting the strain in them.

"Bad night?" she said, leaning close.

"Ummm."

"Which one are you?"

"I'm always me. What happens now is like a drift, a daydream. It's a mask that someone drops over me. If I'm lucky," and Jack leaned back in the chair to look her in the face, "I remember Mom making cookies while I chop vegetables for a salad. Or I'm fighting with my brother or we're getting homework off the tutor. But if I'm not . . . then I'm fighting *sand*."

"Anything I can do to help?"

He inhaled deeply and she knew he was breathing in the fragrance of her hair and skin. The corner of her mouth quirked as he answered, "Nothing that wouldn't make Rawlins awfully uncomfortable."

She pouted at him. "The problem with being one of the boys is that I have to act like one of the boys." She smoothed his hair from his forehead. "It's my watch."

He got to his feet. "Let me know if anything happens."

Amber made no answer but watched him leave the deck. She wondered if he would be any more successful than she at getting some sleep. She sat down in the warm chair he'd just vacated. Constructed for a warrior Thraks, it dwarfed her lithe form. She pressed the back of her hand to her forehead, mopping up a dewy film of sweat. Damn Vandover. She could not sleep, she could not wake from the nightmare, and it took all her discipline to keep from flinching when someone like Jack was near. How could she ever tell him what had happened . . . how could she ever take comforting from him if she could not bear for anyone to touch her. *Dark child*, she thought. *How do you grow in my mind?*

There must be that within her which was very fertile.

She shivered away from those thoughts and forced her attention to the screens and displays as the cruiser arced through nothingness toward somethingness.

Rawlins was on watch when the ship came out of hyperdrive and began braking into the decel-

maneuver known as turning the corner and he was on watch again when Claron came into view. He let out a yell that echoed through the near-empty cruiser, waking Amber and alerting Jack.

Jack put aside the tool he was using on Bogie. The opalescent armor shifted, levering itself to its feet. "What is it, boss?"

"I'd say we've reached Claron. Rawlins'll be putting us into orbit there until we can pick up traces of Colin."

Flexalink shimmered. Did the armor tremble in eagerness? Jack put a hand on the gauntlet.

"I know the way," Bogie said, his deep voice hollow within the battle armor.

Rawlins yelled again, "On deck, sir!"

"I know you do," Jack said soothingly. He disconnected the power lines to his tools. "I'll be back, or you can come up. Just don't break anything."

Under the suit's power, Bogie was like an overgrown, very uncoordinated child. Jack left in answer to the captain's summons without looking back to see if the armor followed him.

He was not prepared for the sight that met him in the control room. Rawlins had boosted the display and put it on the big screen—there it was, the wreckage that had once been a verdant, promising planet. To know that he had been the cause of its destruction had put a lump in his throat before he'd even stepped on deck.

And now this. Cloud cover and oceans—and a tinge of green snaking among the char. Amber was there ahead of him. Her hair streamed loose about her shoulders and there was a glow in her eyes as she reached for him.

"You did this! You did."

"Out of the ashes," Rawlins murmured. "You made them bring it back out of the ashes."

Jack gripped the railing in front of the observation screen. Claron filled his vision—newborn, hopeful, promising yet again. "I didn't do it. The terraformers did. Look at it. Think your parents will apply again?"

Rawlins shook his head. His deep blue eyes looked from Jack back to the screen. "No," he said. "They've resettled. But I just might." He tapped the control back. "I've sent out a new ident . . . they might not be too happy to sight Thraks."

On the heels of his statement, the com board lit up. Rawlins gave Jack a grin and bent his head over the missive, tapping back a quick reply, the keyboard being more reliable than the verbal sending because of Thrakian mechanics.

"Oh, my," Amber said as Rawlins replaced Claron with a deciphered version of the communication. "Such language."

The harshness of the displayed jargon drove the wonderment out of Jack. He *had* done it, in his way. He had been responsible for the firestorming and now he'd made them turn the clock back. An ending, and a beginning.

Rawlins snorted at Amber, saying, "Only a guttersnipe from under-Malthen would even know what most of that meant."

Instead of flaying him alive with his own words, she went as white as if she'd been whipped, shrinking back. Rawlins didn't see her reaction, but Jack did. She recovered quickly, snapping out a retort at the captain who laughed, leaving Storm wondering if he'd seen what he'd seen. Rawlins knew Amber's background, anyone who had been with Jack over the last seven years knew Amber as well, so why should she be bothered?

Vandover, he thought. His fist closed along his thigh. Baadluster was the only one who called her a lady but treated her like dirt. He thought of Baadluster's whispered farewell. Amber had all her deadly skills back. What had she to fear from the Minister of War? There was no one alive who could make Amber fear with the exception of the unseen master for whom she'd originally been trained.

Vandover, he thought again. Why hadn't he seen it? Vandover, who'd replaced Winton as smoothly and neatly as any succession into power he'd ever seen. Winton, who'd ordered retreat on Milos when there had been no need for one, who'd betrayed the Knights into a foul and disgraceful history. Jack had known there'd been other hands besides Winton's in that plot. Baadluster, the link between Winton and Pepys, unseen, uninvolved until Winton's untimely death made it necessary for him to step forward. How could he have been so blind?

"Amber," he said quietly, thinking to draw her aside and share the truth with her, but static began to spew forth and Rawlins clucked his tongue against his teeth, saying, "There's someone who wants to talk to you, Commander."

Finally, he got the com line open. Battle armor filled the big screen, the helmet tucked under the man's elbow, and Jack smiled thinly as he recognized the darkly handsome head of the man who wore it.

"Deñaro. Am I late?"

The Walker militant bared his teeth before replying, "I left little clues for you on the way out, but you didn't stop for them. You came straight here. How did you know?"

"I know Colin," Jack said quietly. Flanking him, both Amber and Rawlins watched the screen intently.

"Ah." Denaro twisted to look off-camera, then back. "Come on down, Jack. We've got a lot to talk about."

"All right. I've got armor this time." Jack said to Rawlins, "Get the coords."

"Yessir."

Amber slipped back to Jack's side as the display went dark. "Let me go down there with you."

How could he trust her, knowing what he did? What if he were right and Vandover was her master now? Guilt and distrust filtered through him. If Amber had fallen into Vandover's hands, it was because he had driven her there. And yet. . . . The thought must have flickered through his eyes, for she shrank away then, with that same whipped look on her face.

Rawlins said, "We all go or we all stay." He stood up from the control board, quiet determination written on his young face.

Surprised, Jack looked at him. Then he nodded. "All right."

Amber said nothing.

Rawlins added, "And we all wear armor."

Jack, whose ribs still felt the knots of recent injuries, nodded a second time.

Chapter 28

Claron still had that edge to its scent, like an exotic spice, and now it was tinged with smoke and another smell, one that Jack breathed in deeply and which brought a smile to his face. It was that of newly turned loam, rich soil, and he knew that Claron was truly reborn. The banks of greenhouses replaced what he had known as a mining and colonial town, but the enterprise was no less raucous. Skimmer traffic patterned the approaching lanes and he wove in and out of it to reach the lot where they'd been directed after berthing the Thrakian cruiser. Amber was sandwiched between the two of them on the skimmer and she was so subdued it was as if she wasn't even there. Clouds of lace-winged, tiny insects billowed up as he brought the skimmer down on a pad.

The windscreen shielded them until they emerged. Then, for a moment, the insects obscured even the target grids of the suits, there were so many of them.

Amber asked in amazement, "What are they?"

"Don't know," Jack answered. "Possibly they give the terraforming microbes a hand."

"Likely they keep them from getting out of hand," Rawlins commented as he got out. The blue sky reflected off his armor like a mirage off flatlands. His visor was on sunscreen and its darkness did not show his face. "It looks good."

Jack agreed. As the cloud of insects spiraled upward and away from the skimmer lot, Jack caught the approach of another war suit. He pivoted to face it dead on.

He saw Denaro, but not Jonathan's hulking form. "Where's Jonathan?"

Denaro pushed his sunscreen up so his face was clearly visible through the visor. "He's in the quonset. He's not well, Storm."

Amber came to life. "Let me see him." She made as if to brush past Denaro, but he caught her. There was a sound of clashing as the two sets of Flexalinks met and ground on each other.

"Not so fast. This is Walker ground. This whole complex," and Denaro waved, "is Walker reserve. If you've come under Pepys' tyranny, you've got no authority here."

"And if I didn't?"

Denaro dropped his glove from Amber's sleeve. "Then we can talk. Follow me in where we can shed suits."

"I'll keep mine on," said Amber stonily.

"They're weapons as well as defensive skins. This is a sanctuary."

Jack shrugged. He motioned Rawlins back to the skimmer. "We're ready to talk when you're ready to be realistic. We're not the ones who kidnapped a patient and blasted our way out of the imperial hospital wing."

"No," Denaro agreed. "But I wasn't the one who put you in a crèche for two weeks. The Thraks did that."

Jack made a half-bow. "I'm holding no grudges . . . yet."

"All right, then. Follow me." Denaro snapped his sunscreen back down, turned in front of Amber and led the way, angling across the complex where patches of lawn were as green and new as spring shoots.

They had to duck to enter the prefab where Denaro led them. Jack eyed the building with interest. It was well thought out and well stocked—and planning boards were covered with sounding diagrams as well as fly-over maps. "Looking for something?"

"No. Initial surveys we always do, given permission. We found norcite on the far side, where there was also some evidence of a Thrakian infestation—burned out nest and *sand* remnants. If Claron hadn't been firestormed, there's a good chance we'd be up to our necks in Thraks now." Denaro indicated a right-hand corridor. "Third room on the left. We'll be a bit crowded in the armor, but—"

"I can stand crowded," Amber said tartly. She swung past him. Inside the building, Denaro put his sunscreen up again and now Jack caught a bemused expression on his face. The Walker had, after all, been the man who'd taught Amber how to use armor, albeit the lessons had been strictly clandestine.

Rawlins and Denaro fetched up against one another ahead of Jack. He watched as they sorted themselves out awkwardly. Both men had been profoundly affected by Colin in their lifetimes, but what a difference there was between them. Denaro, quick-tempered, ambitious, embittered that the passive way of Walker life was endangering their religious survival. Rawlins, quiet, confident, not Walker born or taught, but linked to Colin by the act of healing performed on him.

Denaro finally deferred to the taciturn blond and let him follow after Amber who managed to put a sway and grace even into the walk of a battle suit.

Jack drew Denaro back for a moment. "Is there anything I should know going in?"

"You should know that Jonathan is dying. I don't know what happened to Colin and Jonathan out there, or who took Colin after they separated—"

"I do," Jack interrupted gently. "He came to meet the Ash-farel."

"Shit." Denaro stopped in his tracks. "I knew it—he told me—but I kept thinking that something else must have happened. The Thraks or one of Pepys' freebooters."

"No."

"You can't go after him alone." Denaro locked gazes with him.

Jack smiled and said, "Let me talk with Jonathan first."

The burly aide had shrunken, was now a clammy white shadow of his former self. Amber had shed her helmet and knelt by the simple cot in a room ill-equipped for hospitalization, her gauntlet dwarfing his hand. There were shiny tracks on her face.

Jonathan turned his skull-like face to Jack. "Commander Storm," he said, and his voice husked. "St. Colin had hoped you'd catch up in time to join us."

"I'm sorry I disappointed him."

"You've never disappointed him. He always said you were a man who always tried to do the right thing." Jonathan wheezed. They all shared his struggle to catch his breath. "Denaro said you would come after me . . . I told him there was never any doubt that you would come after me and Colin. But he is a young and impetuous man . . ."

"We all start out that way," Jack said. The praise from Colin had embarrassed him. He questioned Denaro. "How often do ships go back to Malthen or the Dominion—any place with decent facilities?"

"Bi weekly. Next week."

"Make arrangements to leave him behind and see Jonathan is on it."

"Now wait a minute. We got this far, but now the trail is cold—"

Jack felt Bogie's warmth along his shoulders and back. "We don't need Jonathan. We'll find the Ash-farel without him. I'll hold you," and he pointed at Denaro, "personally responsible for any more suffering this man goes through. Do you have room for us at the compound or do I need to check in elsewhere?"

"Here," Denaro got out. "You can stow your gear here. But as far as Jonathan is concerned, he has to stay with us—he's my witness—"

"He's seen enough," Amber said. She got to her feet, eyes alive with her anger. "We got this far without you. We can find St. Colin without you."

Jack saw the expression come and go. That was a prospect that disturbed Denaro. He made a tough decision, then nodded to Jack. "All right. I don't want to see him go any more than you do."

Rawlins left the tiny room, saying, "I'll get the gear from the skimmer." He blocked Denaro's suit for a moment, and when he'd passed, the expression was gone from Denaro's face. But Jack hadn't missed it. Denaro had let the Walker go only because the man's death would avail him nothing.

Jack left Amber with Jonathan and followed Rawlins to the skimmer. The captain worked with short, energetic bursts of movement that Storm knew concealed anger. Jack caught a crate and held it between them.

"What is it?"

The clarity of Rawlins' blue eyes met his own, somewhat faded gaze. "I don't trust Denaro."

"Neither do I—but I want to have him where I can watch him rather than trailing us. All right with you?"

The subtlety of the battle armor was such that Jack could see it echo the relaxation of Rawlins' own body. The captain nodded. "All right." He took the crate from Jack's hands.

Jack would not let Jonathan hear or see the playback of Bogie's records. After dinner, he took them to a soundproofed room that he had Denaro set up and there played back what the suit had documented, limited though it was. Amber let out a long, shivery breath.

"Good God," she said. It fell into silence in the dimmed room.

They had all shed their armor, although Bogie rested on a rack in the corner, his presence a reminder that what they had just heard and seen had happened.

Denaro had a tumbler of the local rotgut in his hand. He sucked it halfway down before saying, "Colin's been around a long time. He's seen and done a lot. What in God's name could have frightened him like that?"

"Whatever it was, that's what we're going after."

"We've no lead. The trail is stone cold—what do you think I've been doing for weeks here? The Ashfarel come and they go. No warning, no tracks. Even the Thraks, who've been fighting them for a century or two, *don't know where they come from.* There's a lot of space we haven't traversed yet. They could even be coming from behind us." Denaro set his glass down in front of him.

Jack leaned forward in his chair. "Changed your mind about coming with us?"

"No. Someone's got to bring back the body." The Walker militant got to his feet. "You said you could point the way. I suggest you be prepared to do it quickly . . . before the rebellion on Malthen spreads."

"Thinking of giving the word?" Rawlins asked, head up, body stilled, poised with the quiet strength of a powerful animal waiting to strike. Denaro didn't seem to notice it.

"Colin has a devoted following. If disinterest from the Triad Throne and, yes, even the Dominion, has cost us his life, and from all indications it may well have, we aren't going to take it."

"Don't threaten us," Amber said. Shadows of fatigue lined her eyes. She scarcely looked at Denaro as he paused in the doorway.

"I don't need to threaten you. I'm just reminding you. We'll want answers in the morning." He turned on his heel and he was gone.

Amber waited until his presence faded from her awareness, then said tiredly, "I wonder what his stake is."

"What it's always been. He wants to take over Colin's job," Jack told her. "Only Jonathan could have prevented it and he's made sure Jonathan's in no shape to do it."

Rawlins got up. "What do you think the chances are he's still alive after that?"

"I don't know. I just think he is. How about you?"

The captain gave a sudden, boyish grin. "Damned if I know. But I think he is, too. We're kind of connected, you know."

"I know." Jack watched Rawlins leave for the room he'd been given.

Amber folded herself up tighter, defensively, in her chair. She retreated to her old habit of hiding part of her face under a wave of her long, golden-brown hair. The unhidden eye stared at him. "Do you really think he's still alive?" she asked finally.

"I do. But I don't know how much longer he's going to stay that way when we find him if I take you with me. What I don't know is how Vandover hopes to trigger you from Malthen."

She flinched. She opened her mouth to say something, then looked away, shut her mouth, and remained silent.

Something was wrenching inside of him. He thought for a moment it was the battle between his two selves, but his thoughts were crystal clear. He fought for a calm breath. His chest felt tight.

"How much," she said softly, looking at her tucked under feet as if contemplation would reveal to her the mystery of life, "do you know?"

"Only that you were desperate enough to reimprint, and that Vandover has his hooks into you. He couldn't do that unless you were afraid of him. You wouldn't be afraid of him unless he's the one who could trigger you."

"And I thought you were an ass-backward country boy." She sighed. "I can't fight him. He feeds on me. Everything I do just adds fuel to him."

"Who's he stalking?"

She shook her head, the movement freeing her pale face from the curtain of hair. "I don't know. Even when he's triggered me, I don't know until it's too late."

"Pepys."

She hid her face in her hands, muffling a sob. "Yes. Jack, I—"

"Who else?"

"The Countess. That's why the Green Shirts didn't rally behind us when the Walkers broke loose."

"What about Colin?"

"I—I don't know." She brought her hands down, wiped her nose on her sleeve, oddly like the girl-child he'd met years ago. "You and I both know it's probable. Colin's death would throw suspicion on Pepys, break him completely—and break the Walkers, too."

"Denaro doesn't have what it takes to take over without bloodshed." Jack reached for his own glass of homebrew, untouched until now. He didn't ask if she had orders to do him in. He didn't want to hear the answer. The liquor went down, burning his throat, anything but smooth. He coughed.

Amber made a rueful face. "I could use a drink. What do you recommend?"

"Anything but this, but this is all we've got." He refilled his glass and passed it to her. "At least it'll help you sleep." The knot in his chest mellowed out. "I can't help you. I can love you, but I can't help you."

Her hand touched his briefly as they exchanged the glass. She looked up. "I think . . . if you love me . . . I can do almost anything. But he's always with me . . . in my thoughts, my dreams, like a blackness grafted onto me. Sometimes I think I'm looking into what Colin calls hell."

"Dig deep and fight it. You were always at my back. Now I'm at yours. I can't help you, but you're not alone. And whatever happens, I won't let you kill Colin."

Her lower lip trembling, she raised her glass to Jack in a salute. Eyes brimming, she downed the liquor. She stifled her cough with the back of her hand. "Now, just how are we going to find him?"

Jack turned and looked at Bogie. "He tells me he's the signpost. Now, Bogie, tell me what you didn't record."

Chapter 29

He was the rose, the attar, with thorns on the inside. They pinioned his soul to flesh that could no longer stand to bear it . . . and they wouldn't let him go.

It made little difference that now the Ash-farel could talk to him, and he could understand. He was pain incarnate in a body that only remotely resembled humankind, that creaked and wobbled when it would stand, that bent when it should be rigid, that wept when it should be dry. He only had peace when he left it and discord when they pulled him back.

His best memories were those of when he'd gone to seminary school, a rough man, too old to be called a boy, a man who had already worked a miracle, and now had to learn the rules and laws governing what he had done. Those were the days, the days when he thought he could accomplish anything by the laying on of hands. Among his schoolmates was a quiet, sardonic red-haired lad who would have been the butt of jokes except that he was from a family of considerable power and had a way of remembering grievances and paying them back later in a sly, undetectable way. The redhead had an earthy intelligence and though he left later for the military school he'd prayed for, Colin and Pepys had gotten along well with one another. The key had been mutual respect.

His fondest memory of the seminary had been his basement room. He was lucky enough to have one with windows, a wall of them, and though they were near the ceiling, they looked out across the lawn. If he stood on a chair, his eyes were level with the grass. If he watched from his normal height, he saw the dirt pressed up against the glass pane, and the roots in that earth as they stretched their tiny tendrils out and thrust forth life from dirt and moisture. Sometimes the dean's little black and white dog would look in at Colin while he studied and bark insulting noises at him as if he were a rat gone underground.

He hadn't thought of those windows in a long time. Yet he knew that they had inspired him a lot during his first, fiery years. People were like seeds and if they could be struck with the right inspirations, they, too, would grow and flourish. He'd spent a lifetime trying to emit enough godspark for nations to thrive on.

In the end, he hadn't done all that much, really. He'd been much more successful in his smaller ambitions. He dreamed now and pondered those windows, with the seeds bursting forth and growing flowers or grass stalks. The Ash-farel were calling him back, he could feel their blasted tugging just when he was about to know why he'd failed. Where he had gone wrong in trying to find the proof he needed that God Incarnate had walked other worlds as well. Why he had failed to provide the right stimulus for the seed of mankind to thrive.

As they pulled him back, memories of other worlds whirled past him ... weeds poking up through broken concrete streets, flowers growing through cracks in rock ... *how odd,* he thought. *How odd I should be seeing these things.*

And then it struck him that each seed carried the godspark inside itself—and would be what it would be. It was not a spark imparted from outside, it came from within. All it needed was encouragement to free itself. *Why, I've been going at it backward,* Colin thought, as they made him become conscious.

Now that he knew, he needed to live. He *had* to live. He reached out for that strange bond he'd made before he'd been taken, his signpost, to guide him.

Bogie heard the call. It stirred him as he'd known it would, striking like wild lightning into his very being. His new flesh quivered, cells swirled in a dervish of activity, cilia stretched forth. And even as the call came to him, he knew he would not answer it.

He could not. The good man had walked into a maw of strangeness and fear ... a maw Bogie would not look into, for fear he'd find himself.

He'd thought about it for a long time. He was not berserker, though similar, and he was not Thraks or Milot. He was not human nor one of the genetically altered humanoid races colonizing planets on the far borders of space. He was either nothing ... or one of the enemy, the Ash-farel. And if he was Ash-farel, his symbiosis with Jack had so changed him that he was still nothing, for there would be nothing else like him in all the universes.

Would Jack destroy him if he knew Bogie was the enemy? He and Jack were warriors. It would be fitting.

But he did not want to be defeated. He wanted to live. He wanted to flesh out his entire body, his soul had been homeless long enough. He wanted to look upon himself as he could look upon Jack and Amber through the suit. As the clarion call came to him, he turned it away.

"It's been days," Amber said. "If Denaro knew the answer was in Bogie, he'd have him scrapped."

"I'm not far from it myself." Jack dropped the printouts he'd been scanning. "He's right . . . the trail is completely cold. The Ash-farel literally drop out of a pocket in the sky and drop back in."

"Meaning what?"

"Meaning their FTL is probably instantaneous. They don't have to accelerate into it or turn the corner coming out of it, signaling their presence. One minute they're here and the next, they're gone."

Amber sat down opposite him. She looked as though she'd gotten some sleep at last, her eyes clearer than he'd seen them in a long time. She had brewed up a batch of an herbal concoction the locals swore was a substitute for tea. It wasn't, but it was hot and wet, with a smoky sweetness. "No wonder we can't fight them."

"No, all we can do is lay down a line of defense and hope they trip over us from time to time. But I'm not convinced we have to fight them. Amber, all the colonies they've hit . . . the land remains intact. Civilization is gone, yes, but the land regenerates."

"Ready to be recolonized?"

"Not that, but what," he frowned and rubbed his lower rib cage, "I'm not sure. But there's more destructive ways to carry on a war. It's the flesh that destroys the land and it's the flesh that they war against."

She looked at him across the rim of her teacup. "You're giving them human motives. From what little we know of them, they're totally alien to us. Jack, if we have to go against them to bring back Colin, you'd better be able to fight."

"I'll do what I have to," he bit off, then buried his anger. Amber wisely said nothing and turned her attention to blowing her tea cool. He shoved himself to his feet and went to the makeshift shop where the suits hung on racks to be geared up. Opalescent Flexalinks shimmered briefly as Bogie stirred.

Old memories resurfaced and for a moment Jack fought his revulsion against the life-form harbored there, and then the moment was past. Now he felt only the cold disappointment that, if Bogie did indeed know the way to Colin, he was hiding it. Before he could approach the armor, steps told him someone was behind him.

"Excuse me, sir," said Rawlins as Jack turned to him. The young captain held a plastisheet in his hand. "We've word that a fairly large contingent of Thrakian ships has come out of hyperspace and is turning the corner to Claron."

"We've been followed."

Rawlins nodded, the shock of his white-blond hair falling over his forehead. "Looks like it."

Jack thought rapidly. There was nothing on Claron for them. The Thraks must be hoping that Jack would lead them to the Ash-farel. "Thank you, Captain."

"Is there . . . anything else?"

"Not for now. I think they'll take up position and wait for us to make a move." If they could make a move. Jack eyed the armor on the racks. "You might alert the locals and let them know that this is nothing hostile . . . yet."

"Yes, sir." Rawlins hesitated.

Jack hid a smile. "Questions?"

"What are we waiting for?"

"We're waiting for the enemy to make a move."

"Which enemy is that, sir? The Thraks, the Ash-farel, or Baadluster?"

Jack let his smile show. "If I knew that, Rawlins, I wouldn't be waiting."

With a shake of his head, Rawlins left the shop room. Jack waited a moment, then approached his armor and sat at its boots, crossing his legs. The Dominion Knights had been an order of mental strength as well as physical. Most of the old disciplines had died out when they'd been disbanded and although Jack had tried to reinstitute them when Pepys had revived the guard, he hadn't been entirely successful. But the old rites were ingrained in him and he sought refuge in them now, breathing deeply.

There was strength in pure thought, just as there was in pure action. There was hope in every breath the body took, just as there was potential victory in every movement. He followed the lines and swoops of his exercises to their conclusion. He opened his eyes.

Bogie had moved a gauntlet over where it curved in the air just above his head. Jack reached up and took the hand in his. "No suit, no soldier," he said. "We've been there and back again. Our last battle is close, Bogie, very close. I'm ready."

He felt the flicker of touch that was Bogie rising to meet him. He was not psychic, like Amber . . . if the alien had not inhabited his armor, he would never have known its thoughts, but he did not regret it.

I have been shamed, Bogie said. *I have run from battle.*

"You've always done all I've asked of you. You've carried me when I was dying, filled me when I was empty. You've been as good a friend as anyone I know."

You gave me life. Now I run from doing the hard thing. A profound sadness tinged the deep, rumbling mental voice.

Jack wondered what bothered the sentience and thought again of the haunting scream Bogie had recorded. Was facing the Ash-farel so terrifying that Bogie could not do the duty Colin had given him—could not be the signpost Colin had intended? "What frightens you?"

Not living. Not fighting. Bogie paused. *Not knowing what it is I am meant to be.*

"Ah, Bogie. At last you know what it is to be human." Jack sighed.

I am not human.

"You might as well be. You're going to have to dig deep for those answers."

Did you . . . dig deep?

"I think so. I'm trying, anyway." Jack got to his feet. "Tell me where Colin is."

I . . . don't know.

"I think you do. I think you're afraid of knowing. Turning away will kill you just as surely as anything else."

Stony silence. Then, *You do not have to search for the enemy. Take off the helmet and look inside. I am the enemy, boss. I am Ash-farel. Your search is over. I have called them to us.*

The corridor filled with the sound of running. Rawlins and Amber hit the shop room at the same time.

"Incoming, Jack. And I don't think we're talking Thraks."

Jack turned. Rawlins had gone pale. "What are we talking about?"

"Out of nowhere, sir. Three of the biggest damn warships I've ever scoped. We're in trouble."

Jack kicked Amber's suit rack across the room. "Get in armor, and then broadcast an alert."

Amber collapsed her suit and opened up its seams. "Claron's got no shields. We're dead in the air unless you've got a plan."

"Let's just get aboard ship and see if we can get off-planet. Then we'll start thinking." Jack grabbed for Bogie. The seams did not open to pressure.

No, boss, Bogie said. *Not this time. I want to become alive. There is no more room for both of us, not enough energy.*

Jack paused, then reached for the hooks holding the suit on the rack and released them. It dropped to its boots with a dull thud. Amber and Rawlins both hesitated, their helmets in their gauntleted hands.

"What are you doing?"

"Nothing. Where's Denaro?"

"Getting defenses up around the compound." Rawlins screwed his helmet into place. "I've got him, sir. He says he'll meet us at the cruiser."

"What about Jonathan?"

Jack slapped Bogie out of the equipment room, saying, "He's better off down here if we're going to decoy them away. Rawlins, get our gear."

The officer left as bid. Amber turned to him. "What's wrong?"

"Bogie won't let me in. He says it'll kill him."

She bit on her lower lip. "Take my suit."

Jack laughed. "I haven't the right curves. Come on, let's go."

"You can't do this. There isn't even a deepsuit aboard that cruiser. Jack, you're in your bare skin. You can't survive any kind of a firefight if we get hit."

"We're not going up there to fight, we're going to find Colin. We don't know why they're here— now get a move on."

She moved, with a string of Malthenian curses that blistered the air.

Chapter 30

"I've got something to tell the emperor," Vandover said, as he stood there at the door, stubbornly blocked by K'rok's massive form.

The Milot's heavy jowls worked as though thinking of forming a word, and his shaggy brows beetled. "No," said the commander.

"It will be of interest to Pepys, I think." Baadluster refused to be intimidated any longer. He could not see his influence waning any further than it already had. He was little more than a prisoner in the obsidite palace.

"No," repeated K'rok.

"You big hairy lump of shit. Go tell his majesty that the Ash-farel are closing in on Claron and see if that interests him enough to talk with me." Vandover's lips tightened into a thin, pale line.

K'rok moved deliberately, shutting a door shield between them as he left his post. Vandover made an inaudible sound and whirled about, pacing the corridor. His hands worked in and out of fists as he strode, his long vested overrobe unfurling in his wake. He heard the *whirr* of servos behind him before Pepys' thin voice.

"Vandover. What is it?"

Baadluster pulled up. Pepys signaled K'rok to

disarm the door shields and drove into the hallway. Much color had returned to his face, and his
aura of hair crackled with energy. But nothing
could be done to restore movement to that portion
of his face frozen by the stroke. Baadluster could
see the butterfly stitches surgically put in to keep
the eyelid from drooping too unpleasantly over his
eye. He cleared his throat to make it appear as if
he had not been staring. Pepys smiled. Vandover
wondered for a moment how many muscles of the
face and even the light of the eye made up that
expression. He also wondered if his own eyes
glimmered pleasantly when he smiled. Somehow,
he doubted it.

"Your sources are better than mine," Pepys per-
sisted. "What have you come to tell me?"

"Only that the Ash-farel have returned to Claron. It appears we no longer have to go in search
of them, they have come to us."

"Bearing Colin, perhaps." Pepys wheeled his
conveyance about. "I wish I could be there." His
voice trailed off. He looked back over his shoulder. "Thank you, Vandover." He disappeared beyond the bulk of the Milot commander's form, lost
once again to Baadluster.

K'rok showed his teeth. He stepped back and
brought the door shield down. Vandover stood
there in frustration. It was clear to him that Amber must be brought back, for she had more work
to do. And the Green Shirts would regret most bit-
terly that they had hesitated to rally to him at this
crucial time. Plotting drove his chin down to his
chest in thought as he left the emperor's quarters.

* * *

The Thrakian cruiser shuddered under them. Bogie's presence loomed on deck while the four of them rocked in their chair-webs as the Ash-farel warship thundered over them, flanked on either side by the other two.

"Come about!" Jack yelled.

Sweat dappled Rawlins' face. "I can't do it, sir. It's not that maneuverable."

"Damn it's not," Storm retorted. He'd seen Thrakian ships in motion, knew that they could fly rings around the warships—but Rawlins was not a Thrakian pilot. Neither, for that matter, was he. "Bring it about any way you can," he amended.

Denaro said, "No fire yet, but they have us targeted."

"No," Amber contradicted. "They have Claron targeted."

Something clenched in Jack's gut. Claron's fragile life would not survive a scourging by the Ash-farel. Not Claron. *"Rawlins, I don't care how you do it, but get us between them and dirtside."* He hadn't come this far to lose.

Bogie, linked to him by the warrior spirit they had in common, felt the fire of his determination. His grids gave him confused readings over the suit cameras. The flooring suddenly gave way under him as the cruiser went into a rollover. The armor went to its knees.

"Hang on," Denaro called, too late for most of them. Amber gave a brief cry as her chair swung about and she was thrown from one side of its webbing to the other, her tawny hair awash about her face as if she were seaborne.

The cruiser slammed forward. Rawlins let out a yell of triumph. "That does it!"

The ship surged past the warships as it flew over them. Denaro muttered to himself, "Watch it, watch it, we're still being targeted by *something* down there."

Their monitors filled with the topside deck views of the ships they were passing. Jack felt awed at the armament he spotted, at the sheer massive power of the vehicles. "I don't think," he said slowly, "that they *have* a home planet. We're looking at a goddamn city, a fortress."

"The Thraks will be happy to hear that." Denaro swiveled in his chair. "Rawlins, can you put a shield up over our ass?"

"I'm steering. You cover our rear if it's so damned important to you."

Jack leaned over the board in front of him. He had done a lot of looking at this board during sleepless nights while coming to Claron. He found a shield button, studied the pattern. He punched one with the heel of his hand. "That should do it."

"Got it," said Denaro. "That should help some." The cruiser rocked suddenly, viciously. "Just testing." Harmless orange fire washed over the screen and reflected upon his face.

"Now they know we've got our defenses up." Jack looked at Amber. "Keep your helmet where you can get to it easily. If anything happens, remember armor can act as a deepsuit."

She turned her golden eyes to him. "We're not going anywhere," she said.

"You wish," Denaro's voice carried a sardonic edge.

Jack looked at his monitor. The warships were gaining on them and fanning out. He knew a flanking maneuver when he saw one. "Rawlins."

"I see it, sir. I don't know how to push this baby any more."

Amber saw it, too. "They're driving us back toward Claron."

"All right, then. Just keep us in between."

"What are we going to do?" Worry, not fear, colored her voice. "They're driving us down."

"We start firing back before that happens. They're not picking up our signal. If they won't listen to our hailing, we'll see if our firepower can get their attention." Jack rubbed his hand over the back of his neck. "Give me a range, Denaro."

"We'll be within Pequena's orbit in five minutes and hit the ionosphere about twenty beyond that."

Pequena was a very small and very close moon. It was about three times larger than the Thrakian cruiser and its proximity made her appear much more prominent on the Claronian horizon than it would have in a more normal orbit. It was too much to hope she'd be on the darkside, away from them. "Where does she lie?"

"We're going to trip over her going in."

"Can you do a slingshot around her?"

Rawlins looked up. His dark blue eyes blinked slowly. "You've been listening to some real hotshot pilots. I don't think Pequena has enough gravity to get ahold of us."

The theory was good, the hope that Pequena's hold on them could slingshot them out of their present course, angling them unpredictably away from the Ash-farel. Not too many pilots he had known would have tried it. Jack smiled. "Just a thought. Okay, we'll use her as a shield, then, if we decide to return fire." He felt Amber's presence behind him, her gauntlet on his shoulder.

"I'm going to find Colin."

"Amber . . ."

"I can do it. Let me try."

Jack closed his eyes briefly, not wanting to make this decision. If she could find him, could she also strike at him? Before he could answer, a strangled noise came from Bogie in his armor.

"Jay-sus," Rawlins said, startled. "What was that?" On top of his exlamation, Denaro cried, "Here's Pequena."

They shot past it so closely they must have kicked up dust on the moon's surface, Jack thought. Its pocked and rilled terrain filled the portside monitors. The vision exploded and the Thrakian cruiser jumped violently as the shock waves hit it. Rawlins cursed as he wrestled with the steering. A thin ping followed by a violent *whoosh* filled the air, and silence followed it as suddenly.

"Leak stopped," Denaro said grimly.

The back cameras displayed the shower of destruction of what had been Pequena. Gravel and dust sprayed out, glowing red with fire. One of those bulletlike rocks had pierced the Thrakian ship. The miracle was that more hadn't.

"Amber, I've got to know which ship Colin is on, *if* he's on a ship. We've got to be able to fight back." Jack truned to Denaro. "Got any gunnery turrets ready?"

"Powering up now," the Walker said.

Amber bent her head. This was a hell of a time to take calming breaths and begin soul-searching. The chair rocked violently about her as more shock waves reached them. She closed her eyes.

Dark child in her mind. Groping, probing, pain

that should be pleasure ... oh, gods, Vandover....
She bit her lip hard, hoping that small agony
would chase away her haunt. Hard, dark eyes
staring back at her ... *you can't escape me, milady....* She couldn't break free of this waking
nightmare, she had no choice but to take him with
her looking for Colin. *Oh, gods, don't make me kill
him....* Amber looked up, wildly, heart pounding.
"Help me," she cried, but her voice stuck in her
throat and the others were too busy to notice. Her
mouth worked without sound.

Then a gauntlet gripped her forearm. The armor pressed close. *I know the way,* Bogie said.
He took her with him.

The contact came with a blazing shock. White
light branded her mind, shearing Vandover away
with its force. For a split second, she thought it
had purged her mind of everything, but then she
saw that, no, it was a beacon and everything stood
out crystal clear. Vandover stood, hunched into
his dark cape at one end of her mind, the light so
blinding that he could be seen only as a shadow,
and at the beacon's beginning was another figure,
squarish, thinning hair ruffled about a mature
face, the clothes that of a mining workman—
"Colin!" she cried out, the name bursting from
her throat.

Her mind went dark. The light gone. Vandover
stilled. Bogie held her arm tightly and she wondered if he had felt what she had. She swallowed
down the lump in her throat.

"I've got him," she said. "Lead ship. In the ...
the middle. Jack, he's alive."

"Damn." Jack came about. "Denaro, shut down
the guns. We can't risk taking the offensive."

"They're bringing us down," Rawlins warned. Screens lit up as they hit the ionosphere and heat shields went up. Claron filled the displays.

"Try to stay away from the installations," Jack said. "We've got some control."

Amber sat back in her chair and took a deep breath. Bogie stayed at her side, silent. The ship spiraled down as its shepherds stubbornly forced it planetward.

"It's going to be a rough landing," Rawlins said. "Belly down."

They braced themselves for the hit. The Thrakian cruiser burst through the clouds, through mist and downward, dragging atmosphere and gravity with it. There would be no mat to brake it, no berthing to cradle it at journey's end, no hope that they could ever land intact enough to take off again. The only hope they had was to survive the landing at all.

"They're coming with us," Denaro warned.

Amber felt the gauntlet on her arm close. Was Bogie frightened? Did he share her sense of mortality? She made a soothing noise that did not finish. It got caught in her tightening throat.

Denaro said, very calmly, "They're coming in firing, Jack. We'll never make it down."

Bogie let out a howl.

Chapter 31

I know the way. Colin froze on the bridge as the words burned into his mind. The Ash-farel had herded him on deck, urged him quietly as he tottered his painful body where they wished him to be.

"We are hunting," they said, and he knew despair. The Ash-farel did not make war, as he knew it. They hunted and eradicated. He knew they might well be hunting his people.

"We have heard a call," they told him. "We are unsure. Listen with us."

And then his thoughts had lit up as if novaed. He reached for Bogie with all his hope and joy, embraced Amber for an incredible moment, lost her but stayed with Bogie, warmth blazing through him as they melded and when a howl of terror eclipsed that joy, the Ash-farel reacted.

The ship's bridge pitched under him. He clung to the shoulder of Na-dara for strength in his physical self as his thoughts interwove with Bogie's fear and desperation.

"I hear," Colin said. And he showed Na-dara what it was he heard, all the while trembling, knowing his friends' lives were being measured in seconds, if he could stop the Ash-farel from hunting, if he could get the Ash-farel to listen to his friends. The screen in front of him filled with the vision of the slender, dwarfed Thrakian vessel as it plummeted groundward toward Claron's new soil.

"If you hear, we also must hear," Na-dara said reluctantly. He reached out to the control board. The tractor beams came on, seizing the Thrakian ship, controlling its rapid descent into a safe landing, and they followed it down, the keels of the warships plowing into the loam.

The Ash-farel turned to Colin. Its saurian face was avid. "You must help us to listen," Na-dara said. "We hear the echo of one of our lost children in your thoughts."

Colin wondered about that. The warship shuddered as its great bay opened. He painstakingly left the bridge and tottered to the tongue of ramp that lowered him to Claron.

Fresh air touched him. There was mist in it, comforting to the burn of his skin. He saw the Thrakian ship pop its air lock, and figures tumble out . . . armored, all of them, except for Jack—Colin's heart swelled at the sight of Storm—and he spread his arms in welcome.

They stared unknowingly at the white-robed figure and then the dark blue armored soldier reached up and took his helmet off. Rawlins said slowly, "My god. It's Colin."

The Walker could have wept, did weep, knowing that someone recognized him, beyond all hope that they could have done so.

* * *

Amber could not tell if it was the Claron mist on her face, or the tears she shed, as she stood back after gingerly embracing Colin. The man in her thoughts and memories did not stand in front of her. She searched for remnants of him in this tortured, elongated caricature of humanity. Only the voice remained the same, and the hair, and the eyes—she did not know how Rawlins had recognized him.

Denaro paced the virgin soil, not caring that his armored boots churned up new seeds and shoots, trampling them. Colin looked at him. "Have a care, my son," he said. "You are being listened to."

Jack had kept his arm about Colin's waist as if knowing instinctively that the older man found it difficult to stand. He looked up the ramp into the darkened interior of the warship. It was cavernous and held secrets. "By them?"

"Yes. You must understand that any attempt at communication at all is miraculous. To them, we are parasites. Vermin. The worlds are better off without us. Would we talk to such creatures, in their position?"

Understanding illuminated Jack's face as Colin spoke. "That explains their warfare."

"Yes. Only they call it hunting."

Denaro stopped short. "Tell them we've come for you."

Colin made an abrupt movement, lost his balance and would have fallen but for Jack's bracing. His face twisted. "Knees don't always lock," he said by way of explanation, then turned to Denaro. "You don't know what you ask. Could I live like this among you? I think not. I see myself mirrored in your eyes. I am a grasshopper of a man

. . . a walking skeleton. My pain numbers my days. But," and he looked at Amber kindly. "The price paid is not without reward. I talk, and they listen."

"They threw a tractor beam on us," Rawlins said. "I think it kept us from splattering the landscape. You did that?"

"I asked. They listened. We were both fortunate." Deliberately, Denaro spat over one armored shoulder. He held his helmet in one glove as if it were a weapon he might throw. "You have obligations."

"You do not need to remind me of my former life."

"I need to bring you back."

The two Walkers stared into one another's eyes. A faint tinge of pink dusted Colin's painfully boned face. "If for no other reason than to pick a successor?" he asked carefully.

Denaro flushed then. "The streets of Malthen run with blood. My brethren chose to fight, but now is not the time. We are wasting good men, good weapons."

Amber felt chilled by his words. Colin made a desultory wave. "I have other matters to settle first. The Ash-farel are listening, and they're growing impatient. Bogie." He turned to the opalescent armor.

I hear you.

"Bogie, there is a good chance that these are your people. They cannot quite hear you, as they put it, but they can listen to you through me. Do you wish it?"

The sentience did not answer immediately. Jack reached out with his free hand and clasped the shoulder of the battle suit. Colin said gently, "I know the way."

There was another muffled howl as Colin swept him up, and Bogie could not fight the torrent of thought as it took him. Without moving a physical step, Bogie and the Walker saint joined the Ashfarel who had been observing them from the shadowy interior of the warship.

He felt their exultation and more, the fierce burning warrior spirits that he knew were kindred to his own, but when he spoke, they did not quite hear. It was only when Colin bridged him that he could touch them, could know that his flesh had once been their flesh.

And the difference that must be spanned was that which he had taken from Jack. He could hear them, but they would not, could not hear him without Colin. He railed at the difference. He was theirs, but not theirs. And finally, in sadness, Bogie pulled away from them and from Colin, knowing that he could not return to them.

He was alone.

No. In his flesh was Jack and Amber, in his spirit, in his thoughts. They made the difference, but they also transformed him.

He would not be alone again.

Colin released him. They stood once again in the misty morning breeze off Claron. Jack's hand touched the Flexalinks which Bogie used as skin and shell both.

"I am," Bogie said, "Ash-farel. And I am not."

Colin's face had grayed with strain. He nodded wearily. He had no chance to turn away as Denaro strode over and snatched him up, tearing him away from Jack. He brought his armored knee up viciously into Jack, knocking him aside.

Colin cried out, "Don't. The Ash-farel—"

Denaro leapt past Amber as she grabbed for him, their armor clashing, and her gauntlet slipping away.

Colin bumped on the shoulder epaulets, his breath torn from him, gasping, "Denaro, you don't know what you're doing—"

The ground fell away from under them. Denaro snarled, "I know the Ash-farel won't touch me as long as I've got you. I need you, old man, just long enough to make a statement in front of witnesses—"

White armor landed in front of them, and Bogie threw up his arms, saying only, "No."

They clashed, Walker and alien, the man hampered by the burden of frail flesh over his shoulder. Denaro kicked out. Bogie turned, catching the boot on his flank. He hit his power vault and returned the blow, staggering Denaro backward. He came back with his fist and their armor pealed out as they made contact. Denaro shook himself loose of his burden, throwing Colin away, heedless of the white-robed figure tumbling away from him.

He brought his gauntlet up and fired, laser wash scouring Bogie's chest and helmet. Amber ran to Colin's side and knelt over him, protecting his body with her own armor. Bogie reeled, straightened, and jumped at Denaro. They bowled over and then Denaro shook free.

Rawlins helped Jack stand. Jack fought to breathe, winded. He felt broken in two or three different spots. He managed to gasp down some air and his diaphragm loosened slightly. He looked up. He launched himself across the broken field at Amber.

Rawlins saw what Jack saw even as the man dove at Amber and Colin to protect them. Denaro, at close range, cocked his wrist to fire, heedless of the damage the backwash from a wrist rocket would do. The white armor was his sole target, his obsession.

He fired. The rocket exploded, taking the white armor dead on. It staggered back, flowering open, Flexalinks splitting. Rawlins unhooked his helmet and screwed it on, as Denaro began to pivot toward the three huddled on the ground just as the explosion washed over them. The ragged hem of Colin's robe caught fire spontaneously. As the orange flames gouted upward, Jack smothered them with his body.

Rawlins hit his vault. He smacked into Denaro just below the shoulder. Before the armored Walker could right himself, Rawlins locked his arm about the man's upper torso, and tore the helmet off. Denaro yelled in fury.

His shout was cut short as Rawlins reached in and broke his neck.

The battle suit slumped over in response to its wearer's death. Rawlins dropped back to the ground. He tore his own helmet off.

"My God," he said, as if unsure himself just what he'd done. He stumbled to Jack's side as he levered himself off Colin's body.

The Walker saint lay crumpled, his robes sooty and stained. His broken form looked as if it had finally taken all the punishment it could. Amber let out a sob. Rawlins fell into a kneeling position beside his friend's body. The pallor of his face matched the winter-wheat color of his hair, Jack thought. Aloud, he said, "You did what you could. It's too late, that's all." And he wondered who the Ash-farel would listen to now, if indeed they would listen at all.

Thunder rolled sullenly in the sky. Rawlins caught his breath and reached for Colin's hand.

What happened next, neither Jack nor Amber could be sure, nor could they ever describe it except to say that the gauntlet took on a glow, an infusion of light and dark as it met Colin's flesh. Rawlins never saw it, for the tears obscured his dark blue eyes. He held the dead saint's hand for a long moment and when he let go, the radiance faded. The spicy air of Claron filled with an aroma that made Amber think of roses.

With a deep, shuddering sigh, Colin rolled over and sat up. They could see life shimmering into him, through him. He reached for Rawlins' hands. "My boy," he said. You have returned the gift I gave to you."

Rawlins' mouth dropped open. Then, he shook his head. "I'm no Walker."

"No? Well, then, I'm sure we can find someone who will teach you. But a good man is a good man, a saint is a saint, regardless of his religion. If my Walkers won't accept you, there will always be those who will. You'll do." Colin released his gauntlets and looked at his own hands briefly. "You took away my pain. That'll make listening with the Ash-farel a little easier."

Jack looked up. He frowned. "If there are any

left. Rawlins—that's reentry rumble! The Thraks are coming in! And the Ash-farel are on the ground—Amber, get Colin up and in the ship. We've led them into a trap."

Chapter 32

Vandover sat in his com net, face furrowed with anger. Amber had been able to brush him away, but he'd sifted through her mind well enough to know that the team had found Colin, been in touch with him. He would not be turned away from his goal now. She would do his will.

He took a cleansing breath. He knew her well, he did, the silken feel of her skin, the curves and valleys of her body as well as the twists of her mind. With every heartbeat, he drew closer to her again and she would be his. . . .

"What are you doing, Vandover?"

The minister jerked upward in his chair. He looked at Pepys, weakened, hapless Pepys, and smiled even as he sent his questing thoughts out farther, closer to his quarry. He made a steeple out of his hands. "I do my work, emperor."

"You've been relieved of your duties." It was night on Malthen, and the emperor had been asleep. Lines from his pillow still creased his face and his frizzy red hair was matted down. He ran his good hand through it as if aware of Vandover's observation.

"Not all of them, I'm afraid. Not my duty as I see it."

The cables and wires of the com net prevented Pepys' scooter from bringing him closer. The emperor remained in the doorway, frustrated. His anger showed on his face. "What are you doing?"

Vandover smiled that humorless smile of his. "A little long-distance assassination, my dear Pepys. The cease fire you've instituted won't last long when the Walkers discover what you've done to their much beloved saint."

"They've found Colin?"

"Oh, yes. And the Ash-farel. And," he smiled with real satisfaction now as he found Amber's mind and sunk his hooks mercilessly into her, "I have found them." He laughed dryly. "Remember the east wing? Remember the quorum of psychics you used to keep ensconced there, just in case one of them could sense or predict something for you?" He leaned forward, the comnet trailing about his head like an obscene tiara. "Well, my dear emperor, you've had the genuine article under your nose for years without a clue. She's beautiful and deadly—but she's mine."

Pepys' mouth worked silently. He saw his soul suddenly stretched out before him and knew that the stain of Colin's death was a stain he could not bear upon it. He had to stop Vandover even if he had to kill him to do it. He tried to thrust himself from his conveyance.

They left their wounded and dead upon the field. Rawlins shut the Thrakian cruiser after them, Amber strangely pale as she helped Colin into a webbed chair. Jack climbed above, into the overhead turret. The cruiser vibrated into life.

Colin said, "Since this is a Thrakian vessel, I presume you can open channels for me?"

"Yes, sir, but—"

The Walker leaned his head back against the molded chair. He looked above. "Jack, hold your fire."

Jack looked at the Thrakian warships coming in lean and mean on his grid. "Guthul won't let us go. I don't know what you have in mind—"

"Norcite. The Ash-farel know far more about norcite than you and I ever will. I think the Thraks will trade our lives for the location of additional deposits."

Jack came about in the turret, staring down. Amber sat in her chair next to Colin. The shock of all they'd gone through was written in tiny lines about her eyes and mouth. She gave him a stricken look.

Giving norcite to the Thraks was like giving weapons to a baby. Even if it meant bargaining for his life now, it also meant he would spend the rest of his life fighting Thraks and *sand*, until Tricatada gave out and her generation died fighting his—

"Shit." The realization hit him.

Colin jerked in his chair. "What is it?"

Jack began to slide out of the turret. "Open up that channel, Rawlins. I've got something better to trade."

An explosion rocked the cruiser. "Close," said Rawlins. "They're getting our range." He opened up the monitors. They showed one of the Ash-farel vessels beginning to lift off.

Jack faced the screen. "Guthul, I know you're on-line."

The screen came to life with the Thraks' Kabuki mask looming fiercely at him. "I am, Commander, and this time I will find victory and honor!"

"There's honor for all of us, but only if you call a cease-fire." He looked to Colin. "Can you keep the Ash-farel from fighting back?"

The man looked bemused. "I can," he answered slowly, "try."

Amber shuddered.

Jack faced Guthul's visage again. "I know," he said, "the answer to Tricatada's infertility. I think our lives are worth that, don't you?"

The mask reformed slowly. Then, "You trick us."

"No. But I won't tell you if we're under attack."

"You have allied with our ancient enemy . . ."

Jack shook his head. "The Ash-farel don't need us and they don't need you. Fire on us and you've signed your own death warrant. Do you want fertile eggs or not?"

Behind him Rawlins cautioned, "One of the Ash-farel ships is up. We're on borrowed time."

As if he'd heard him, the Thrakian general bowed abruptly. "We will talk."

Colin let out his breath abruptly. He said, "The Ash-farel are listening. They will allow Guthul's ship to land. The others must, however, pull back."

Vandover laughed as Pepys fell from the scooter. His weakened wrist doubled under him. It broke with a dull pop. The emperor let out a squeak of pain and writhed on the floor. Baadluster spoke and his words dripped venom. "Do you think to stop me now? You should have thought to do it years ago when you still held power." He threw his head back and closed his eyes, discounting the broken emperor across the room.

Pepys closed his lips tightly upon his whimpering. Quietly, so as not to warn Vandover, he began to crawl across the floor.

They met on the valley floor. Jack recognized the land with a shock—it had once been the lush Ataract forest, where he'd done much of his rangering when Claron was still verdant, and now the blast of the landing vehicles had welded the new soil into glassy fields. As he strode over the obsidian surface to the ramp of the Ash-farel vessel, Guthul's contingent waited for him. Amber leaned on him, her breath rasping as she fought to keep pace with him. They had shed their armor. Colin thought it best. He tottered alongside Jack. Only Rawlins wore his suit, and he carried Bogie's remains in his arms. He laid the shattered armor down on the ramp as they came to a halt.

Guthul twisted about. Jack knew Thrakian masks well enough to recognize an expression of pure hatred. Before the Thraks could speak, the Ash-farel finally emerged from the cavernous belly of their ship.

Jack had seen them before, their mummified remains on a dead moon mining colony, in a Walker dig on Colinada, and now in the flesh. They were saurian, immense, and yet curiously avian; they were quick and their scales brilliantly colored. They were three times his size and their eyes were large, and knowingly arrogant. But they were listening.

He could not speak directly to them. Only Colin

could translate what he would say now, so he turned to his old friend as Guthul made impatient chittering noises. Seeing the face of his ancient enemy did not seem to impress the Thraks.

"I can give you only the reason, not a solution. But if we can create a true alliance between us, I can promise you we'll help with the solution."

Guthul and his aides rattled their armor. "Empty words are like empty egg sacs. Flaunt them and we will return to our vessels." He pointed his mask up the ramp to where the Ashfarel milled about. "We will leave the field to fight another day."

"If I give you the reason, you'll come to treaty?"

Guthul bowed. "So my queen has ordered me."

Jack smiled wryly. That was as good as he was going to get from the Thraks. "All right. Norcite has been among the Thraks for a long time. It's a strengthening agent, highly prized for its effects upon armor."

Guthul nodded and said warningly, "You waste my time."

"No. Not by half. When you first began to contend with the Ash-farel, you needed norcite to protect yourselves. At the beginning, you painted it on. It did well. Then, some time ago, you discovered the virtues of ingesting it. Drinking or eating it . . . it not only increased the strength of your armor, but its size. You began to develop your warrior classes and your warfare against your enemies. The end result of all the fighting was a drop in population. Your queens, of necessity, began to work harder laying eggs. You swarmed, taking over whole planets for *sand* nests to hatch and feed those younglings."

The general's mandibles worked. He rumbled, "The enemy knows enough of our secrets.

"But it's no secret now. Tricatada cannot lay a fertile egg. You've come as far as you can. In the last thirty years, you've gone through a frenzy of swarming, driven out of your own lands by the Ash-farel and conquering ours. The Ash-farel have long known of your uses of norcite—every deposit we've found, the two of you have fought over. This has been revealed in archaeological records as well as in present history. But what you didn't know, Guthul, was that it was not the warfare dooming you. It was the norcite. *Norcite makes you sterile.* The warrior class cannot fertilize the queen. Oh, she can lay eggs from now until the stars grow cold, but there isn't a mate alive who can finish the job."

"I am not impotent!"

Jack stared at the enraged Thraks who towered above him. He blinked. "I don't doubt it—but you can't give the queen fertility, either. Maybe only the lowliest Thraks, those never allowed to consume norcite still carry the ability. Maybe not. That answer I can't give you. I can only tell you what happened."

Guthul rattled his chitin in deafening agitation. "Our enemies will destroy us!"

Colin moved forward. "No," he said. "They are listening, and they have compassion. I think I can say. . . ." He trailed off, a quizzical expression on his face. He pivoted very slowly toward Amber. "Amber, what are you—"

Jack saw it in her face, in the intense struggle suddenly imprinted on her features. He jumped and brought her down, their bodies hitting the metal ramp, she fighting him like a wild thing.

"Don't," he begged. "Don't do this. Listen to me, not Vandover. Love, listen to me!" He bore her body down with his and took her face between his hands. Her eyes went wild and she screamed in fury at him.

Colin put his hand to his temple. He closed his eyes in sudden pain.

His arm hurt as if he'd been knifed. He held his breath for fear of whimpering too loudly. He crawled another foot upon the floor. He was close enough now to touch the edge of Vandover's over-robe. To smell the sweat of the man's booted feet. Pepys wrinkled his nose. All those years, and he'd never noticed how Baadluster's feet stank. He pulled himself forward again. With a sudden up-heaval, he wrapped his good hand in Vandover's robe and pulled himself to his knees. Vandover exploded in snarling hatred and the smaller man saw his death in those flat, dark eyes.

Jack stroked her heated face, feeling her body heave under him, not caring if all the Thraks and Ash-farel in the universes saw him struggle with her. "Dig deep," he told her. "I'm here. Fight him. Don't give in. I'm with you."

Rawlins let out a shout and caught Colin's top-pling body. The saint said weakly, "I'm all right. Help Amber." The Ash-farel let out the first sounds he'd heard them make—it was like whale-song. He understood nothing they said and he thought that perhaps he couldn't even hear all that they sang and boomed. Amber thrashed under him again, and a tear leaked out from her eyes.

"Jack," she rasped. "Don't lose me."

"Never."

She shuddered, her eyes rolling back until he could only see their whites. She cried out, "Dark child!"

Pepys screamed as Vandover shook him like a broken doll. He heard K'rok's thundering voice, "What be happening here!" as the Milot leaped over the scooter and into the room. The impact of their bodies sounded like the clash of giants as Baadluster dropped him, forgotten. The hairy Milot and the black-clad man jointed in battle, the com net tiara trailing a tail of sparks as it tore loose. A powerknife buzzed to life in Vandover's hand.

Blood splattered Pepys. He wiped it from his cheek and look up, to see the Milot dripping upon him as the knife cut him yet again. K'rok snarled in outrage, reached out, and punched Vandover in the chest. There was a sickening crunch of bone. Baadluster staggered back, gasping. He clawed at his chest and the powerknife dropped to the floor where its blades whirred angrily. He looked at Pepys as he sank to his knees. His pasty complexion turned purple. Then Vandover collapsed face first, burying the knife to its hilt in his shattered chest.

K'rok lifted Pepys to his feet. The emperor clung to him as if to life itself.

Bodiless, Vandover's thoughts clung to their foul anchorage in Amber's mind. She gasped and bucked as Jack's words made their way to her. She thought of the light Colin had made in her once, the light that had driven Baadluster out. She had to make such a light now.

"Together," Jack said.

She looked into his eyes. He loved her. She had lost him and gotten him back. "I won't let him have you," he told her.

If he only knew. If she did not burn Vandover from her mind now, she would be forever possessed.

"I love you!" she cried. He kept her face between his hands and his eyes became her world. Eyes of rainwater blue. Eyes she had once told someone could never lie. He loved her back.

Happiness roared up like a fire fed by the look in those eyes. It spewed its light throughout her and Amber let it burn.

With a howling, that dark child which was Vandover burned out and was gone.

Chapter 33

"If they can take a man apart and put him back together, it stands to reason they can do the same to armor," Colin said. He smiled at the gleaming opalescent suit standing before them with the radiance of a newly born sun. "And as for Bogie, the suit did its job. It protected the life within it."

Jack smiled. Amber stood within the cradle of his arm. The Ash-farel had dressed her, decorating her like some wild exotic creature, silks and feathers and beads about her. "I wish you'd reconsider coming back with us."

Colin tilted his head. He had the look of the Ash-farel about him when he did it. "No," he answered. "I've passed that robe to Rawlins. He'll do much better than I. I've told him a few of the hard things I've learned along the way. He's got a head start on the job."

Rawlins ducked his head, suddenly and embarrassingly humble.

"Forget Rawlins. I can use your help dealing with Pepys and K'rok."

"My friend. There is no one who can do what I can do here. Even Bogie cannot. But with your help, he will. You've brought the Thraks to bay and you'll have the time you need to rebuild. The

Ash-farel are listening, and that is no small feat. I'd say you've more than met the challenges Pepys handed you."

Jack shook his head. "I was given a job. I did my best. Denaro—"

"You couldn't help him any more than you could save Vandover from himself. Pepys has dismantled his throne, K'rok has his regency over Milos, my Walkers await Rawlins. You've done well. The only thing I regret," and Colin put a finger to his lips as he smiled, "the only thing I regret is not being able to give the vows to bond you two officially."

Amber laughed. "What's stopping you?"

"What? Here and now?" Colin looked about him. The Claron sky was midday bright and clear. The warships perched like gigantic nesting birds and Amber stood among the warriors, a brilliant rainbow-hued nestling.

"We're among friends," she said. "There's no time better. Is there?"

Jack cleared his throat. "Now I know what Pepys felt like with K'rok staring him down the throat demanding a regency." He smiled. "Go ahead, Colin. Do your worst."

It was fitting, Jack thought, to begin again on Claron.

DAW

Cosmic Battles To Come!

Charles Ingrid

DAW

Exciting Visions of the Future!

W. Michael Gear

☐ **STARSTRIKE** (UE2427—$4.95)
The alien Ahimsa has taken control of all Earth's defenses, and forces humanity to do its bidding. Soon Earth's most skilled strike force, composed of Soviet, American and Israeli experts in the art of war and espionage find themselves aboard an alien vessel, training together for an offensive attack against a distant space station. And as they struggle to overcome their own prejudices and hatreds, none of them realize that the greatest danger to humanity's future is right in their midst. . . .

☐ **THE ARTIFACT** (UE2406—$4.95)
In a galaxy on the brink of civil war, where the Brotherhood seeks to keep the peace, news comes of the discovery of a piece of alien technology—the Artifact. It could be the greatest boon to science, or the instrument that would destroy the entire human race.

THE SPIDER TRILOGY

For centuries, the Directorate had ruled over countless star systems—but now the first stirrings of rebellion were being felt. At this crucial time, the Directorate discovered a planet known only as World, where descendants of humans stranded long ago had survived by becoming a race of warriors, a race led by its Prophets, men with the ability to see the many possible pathways of the future. And as rebellion, fueled by advanced technology and a madman's dream, spread across the galaxy, the warriors of Spider could prove the vital key to survival of human civilization. . . .

☐ **THE WARRIORS OF SPIDER** (UE2287—$3.95)
☐ **THE WAY OF SPIDER** (UE2318—$3.95)
☐ **THE WEB OF SPIDER** (UE2396—$4.95)
